"What the—" Suddenly something dashed out of the yard. Bobby didn't get a good look at it, considering it was pretty dark. But whatever it was, it was moving pretty fast and hugging the ground.

It was an animal. Bobby was certain of that. It ran on two legs, its long head held low, its jaws stained with blood. Also, it was big. It looked to be about six feet long, and sleek.

It was also a dark color, scaled and fanged.

Bobby felt his blood running as cold as ice.

It was gone in a second, swallowed up by desert shadows. All Bobby could hear was the drumming of the starlight and the panicked hammering of his own heart. *Could he have seen what he saw?* It made no sense. But he was convinced of one thing:

It had looked just like one of those raptors from *Jurassic Park.*

A *dinosaur. . . .*

The Outer Limits™

A whole new dimeneion in
adventure . . .

THE OUTER LIMITS™

THE INVADERS

JOHN PEEL

Tor Kids!

A TOM DOHERTY ASSOCIATES BOOK
NEW YORK

This is a work of fiction. All the characters and events portrayed in this book are either products of the author's imagination or are used fictitiously.

THE OUTER LIMITS #5: THE INVADERS

Cover art by Peter Bollinger

A Tor Kids Book
Published by Tom Doherty Associates, Inc.
175 Fifth Avenue
New York, NY 10010

Tor® is a registered trademark of Tom Doherty Associates, Inc.

ISBN: 0-812-59068-6

First edition: February 1998

Printed in the United States of America

0 9 8 7 6 5 4 3 2 1

For Ken Boone

In the vast lengths of time, many species have evolved on planet Earth. Some, like cockroaches and sharks, live for hundreds of millions of years. Others, like man, have existed for considerably less time. Over the course of geologic time, many species have been born, lived and perished. It is part of the way of the natural world. Some species have been wiped out by others. The human race has eradicated several hundred species. Natural events have destroyed many more.

Of one thing we can be sure, however: extinction is forever.

Or . . . is it?

CHAPTER 1

"HEADS UP, HERE comes trouble!"

Alyssa Baker glanced up, and then stood, flexing her aching back and her strained calf muscles. Bending down, clearing dirt and sand from an exposed dinosaur vertebra played havoc with her muscles, and she was almost glad of the excuse for a break.

Almost.

She removed the hat that she had to wear to protect her blonde hair from the burning of the South Dakota sun, and smiled slightly at the cheery fake sunflower attached to the brim. Then she replaced the hat and studied the desert through her Ray-Bans.

It was Denby's mob again. Alyssa had suspected it would be. In their humvee, barrelling across the sands. Alyssa sighed. Two months in South Dakota with her best friend, Caitlin Weiss, digging up dinosaur fossils had sounded like fun until a week ago. That was when they'd arrived here, just outside the aptly named town of Furnace, South Dakota. Then reality had set in.

Calling Furnace a town was being generous: it was a collection of about twenty houses and one general store-gas station. There were only about fifty people in town, which was dying slowly of attrition as the young people moved away to somewhere more interesting and with actual job opportunities. The people left in Furnace were as old, dry and baked as the land they lived on.

Except, somewhere in the foothills was a group of militia—survivalists, led by a man named Denby. They didn't like anything to do with the government, and since the dinosaur dig was sponsored by the University of Michigan, that was way too close to government interference in their territory for them. As a result, at least every other day, Denby and some of his supporters would turn up to cause trouble. Nothing too serious, so that they wouldn't run afoul of Sheriff Gates, and maybe the FBI, but enough to let the team know they weren't wanted here.

With a roar of the humvee engine and then a squeal of brakes, the vehicle ground to a dusty halt just alongside the working group. Alyssa looked at Caitlin, who brushed out her own short red hair and grinned back. Caitlin's father, Dr. Sam Weiss, barely kept his temper as he strode across to the humvee. There was a loud bark, and a huge dog leaped at the window. Dr. Weiss jumped hastily back.

Denby clambered out of the driver's seat. He was dressed in his ubiquitous mock-military fatigues, and hat pulled down over his close-cropped graying hair. He looked like a poor man's Arnold Schwarzenegger, and acted like he thought he was the real thing.

''I hear you've been lying about me to the sheriff again,'' he snapped at Dr. Weiss.

Caitlin's father drew himself up to his full height—a good six inches shorter than Denby—and tried to look intimidating. Alyssa liked Dr. Weiss, but she had to admit that his attempt to look imposing was a miserable failure. "I've done nothing of the kind," he replied.

"You accused my boys of breaking some of your trash," Denby stated.

"No." Dr. Weiss shook his head. "I said that one of my artifacts was broken, and that it was most likely that the culprit was one of your men."

"Same thing," Denby grunted.

"It is not," Dr. Weiss insisted. "It's a suspicion, not an accusation. I don't have enough proof to press charges."

"You don't have squat," Denby retorted. "Because none of my boys did a thing. Freeman!" he called, without looking around.

The back door to the humvee opened, and a tall youth clambered out, his hand wrapped in the chain about the neck of what looked like a small bear, but had to be merely an immense dog. "Yes, sir!"

"Any of you boys been messing about in this here camp?" asked Denby, still staring at Dr. Weiss.

"No, sir!"

Alyssa couldn't help giggling. The kid named Freeman was trying to sound so much like a soldier. He wore similar fatigues to Denby, down to the hat and pistol as his belt. Freeman caught the sound and turned to look at her. His eyes widened slightly, and he gave her a careful looking over.

"Though I have to admit," Freeman added, "it does look kind of interesting."

Alyssa grinned, knowing what he meant. Well, she *was* dressed in short shorts, a halter top and about a three-inch thickness of sun block. Alyssa knew she looked good, and didn't mind the compliment.

"Keep your mind on duty, soldier," Denby snapped, but not until he'd looked himself. Then he said to Dr. Weiss: "Maybe one of these . . . assistants of yours broke it. They don't look too well-trained to me."

Dr. Weiss sniffed. "My staff is too competent to be so clumsy. Besides, it looks like someone took a hammer to it."

"Maybe I could take a look?" Denby suggested. "Unless it's classified materials, of course."

Caitlin's father frowned, obviously expecting a trap of some kind. Still, he could hardly refuse. With a curt nod, he said: "Come along," whirling to head for the storage tent. Denby followed behind.

Caitlin nudged Alyssa. "Let's go talk to this Freeman," she suggested. "He's about the only boy around here."

"Boy soldier," Alyssa replied, amused. Trust Caitlin to want to chat this kid up; she'd been working on the three boys in camp. They were all third-year college students, and thought that fifteen-year-old girls were a bit beneath their dignity. But not their wolf whistles. She followed her friend to where Freeman was standing, virtually at attention, still holding the dog.

Alyssa bent forward to greet it, and Freeman seemed to spring to life. "I wouldn't do that, ma'am," he said. "Horse don't take kindly to strangers."

"Horse?" Alyssa repeated. "You call your dog *Horse*? Well, he's got the size for it . . ."

"Short for Crazy Horse, ma'am," Freeman answered. "*He* fought for freedom, too."

That figured—more paranoia. Ignoring the warning, Alyssa bent again and stroked Crazy Horse. The dog almost purred. "I've got a way with dumb animals," she explained, looking up to see him staring at her. Her figure? Or that she could pet his savage guard dog? Either way, Alyssa was amused.

"Can you chat while you're on duty?" asked Caitlin, not wanting to be left out. "Or are you supposed to be playing soldier?"

"It ain't playing, ma'am," Freeman answered. Was he blushing faintly? "We always have to be on duty, ready in case of trouble."

"Trouble?" Caitlin laughed, and gestured around. Aside from the dozen or so tents of the expedition, and the various members of the team, there was nothing but desert. "Are you expecting alien invaders, or something?"

He definitely blushed this time. "The government could move against us any time," he said, sincerity in his voice. "We have to be continually ready, ma'am."

"Why would the government come after you?" Alyssa asked. "Have you been misbehaving?"

"No, ma'am," Freeman answered. "But they just want to take away our freedoms. Anyone who stands up for their rights, the bureaucrats want to take down."

Caitlin snorted. "Rights? You mean carrying guns and playing at soldiers? If you don't like the military, why do you pretend to be a part of it?"

"It's no pretense, ma'am," he answered. "And we're militia, not military. There's a difference. Militia belongs to the people and answers to the people. Military belongs to the powers that be, and answers to them. They ain't accountable."

It made no sense to Alyssa, but she had a hard enough time figuring out the normal sort of boys, let alone one like this. "I wish you'd stop calling me *ma'am*," she complained. "You make me feel like I'm sixty years old and in need of a cane to stand straight. My name's Alyssa, and this is Caitlin.''

''I'm not allowed to fraternize on duty, ma—'' he clamped his mouth shut. Alyssa and Caitlin both laughed at him, and he blushed again.

''So,'' Caitlin asked, ''is Freeman your first name or your last name? Or your only name?''

''First name,'' he replied. ''My folks named me that because that's what they wanted me to be—a free man.''

Alyssa snorted. ''Then I should have been named Corporate Lawyer Baker,'' she said.

''And I'd be Famous Paleontologist Weiss,'' added Caitlin, laughing.

''You're making fun of me,'' Freeman complained.

''I never make fun of a man with a gun,'' Alyssa assured him.

He looked offended. ''I'd never use that on you,'' he said. ''It's for defense, not attack. And I'd never attack anyone as pretty as you, anyway.'' He blushed again.

Alyssa was starting to like Freeman. Oh, he was as loopy as the other survivalists, but he was also sort of charming. ''Why don't you relax?'' she suggested, scratching Horse under the chin. ''Even your savage guard beast can chill out a bit.''

''He shouldn't,'' Freeman complained. ''Don't do that to him. If the colonel finds out, he'll be mad.''

''Colonel?'' Caitlin asked. ''So Denby was in the military once?''

''It's an honorary title, bestowed upon the colonel by his men,'' Freeman explained. ''We're a democratic group, and ranks are voted on by the company.''

''Does Horse get a vote?'' Alyssa asked. He almost answered before he realized that she was joking, and clammed up again. Alyssa smothered a giggle. He really was quite fun, she realized, definitely the most fun she'd had since she'd arrived in Furnace. She was about to talk to him again, when she heard raised voices. It was Dr. Weiss and *Colonel* Denby returning. She supposed she really shouldn't tease Freeman in front of Denby. She didn't want to get him into trouble. Reluctantly, she stepped back from Horse. The dog strained to get closer to her, but Freeman held him back. "You *could* come and see us when you're off duty," she suggested. Then she turned her back on him to look at the two adults.

They'd obviously been arguing about the broken dinosaur egg. It was spherical and about six inches across. It looked more like a fossilized ball to Alyssa than an egg. Dr. West had suggested that it might be the egg of a large dinosaur. The real puzzle was *which* dinosaur. It didn't resemble any fossil they'd seen before. Early this morning one of them had been found shattered. Dr. Weiss had gone into town and complained to the sheriff. Sheriff Gates had obviously been out to speak with Denby.

"It's all pure foolishness," Denby was saying. "I'll admit that we'd like you out of here, Weiss. But breaking your stupid relics isn't our style."

"Our work is important," Dr. Weiss answered. "We could be on the brink of one of the greatest discoveries in paleontology!"

"Your work ain't worth squat," Denby said dismissively. "There's nothing worthwhile to be learned from the far past. Only the recent past. The *human* past. Get your nose out of the dirt, egghead, and live in reality for a while."

"Reality?" Dr. Weiss barked, furious. "You wouldn't know reality if it bit you on the rump! Running around all day playing soldiers and praying for society to break down so that you can take charge. We're not the ones out of touch with the real world.''

''Dream on,'' Denby answered. ''When the apocalypse comes, you and the likes of you will be dead, because you don't know how to survive. Dinosaur bones won't help you survive urban decay, a growing crime rate and the collapse of global civilization.'' He wrinkled his nose in disgust. ''Get back to your toys; me and my boys have more important business to take care of than harassing you.''

''If that's true,'' Dr. Nathalie West called, ''then why are you here and not off shooting at jackrabbits or something else that's never harmed you?'' She strode across to the group from the tent in which she'd been working. Her hands were still caked in the plaster she used to seal the samples for transport.

''I'm just off, ma'am,'' Denby said, touching his hat politely.

''Good,'' she said rudely, but to the point. Her long, dark hair was escaping from her baseball cap, and she was obviously dying to push it back and couldn't. Alyssa liked Dr. West. She was a lot more human than Caitlin's father, and quite a lot of fun at times. But she was also very nononsense. Alyssa figured a lot of it had to do with being a woman scientist. It was pretty much common knowledge that scientists were chauvinists. It seemed like Dr. West was always having to prove herself. Alyssa knew what *that* was like.

Denby gestured to Freeman, who ushered Horse into the back of the humvee and climbed in himself. Alyssa caught him giving her and Caitlin a quick glance. She hoped he'd be back. It was fun having another person her own age to talk to. Caitlin was her best friend, but sometimes she got on her nerves. For one thing, Caitlin was very competitive when it came to boys. Alyssa could almost hear Caitlin purring in anticipation of Freeman's return.

Denby climbed into the driver's seat and sent the vehicle off into the desert again, churning up a cloud of sand and dust to in his wake.

"Enough rest," Dr. Weiss called to the students, clapping his hands. "Let's get back to work, everyone."

The students went back to their bones. Alyssa sighed, ready to get cramped muscles again. Then a different urge hit her. "I'm going to the bathroom," she said to Caitlin. "Back in a minute."

Heading across the site, Alyssa aimed for the latrine tent. It stood off from the rest of the camp a short distance, for obvious reasons. A couple of holes would be dug out every few days, and then filled in and the tent moved. It was way more primitive than Alyssa had ever expected. She'd been rather hoping for trailer homes or something, but apparently such things weren't in the budget. She supposed they were lucky to have shower tents rigged up, so they could at least wash themselves a couple of times daily. Alyssa liked the comforts of home, and missed them rather badly. Pits in the ground was way too survivalist for her liking.

On the way back, she stopped, suddenly, puzzled by something. The ground around here was barren for miles. Even using irrigation, the folks in Furnace couldn't grow much. She'd not seen a plant since she'd been here. The sun just burned anything living right off the face of the planet.

Close to the tent, however, in a small patch of shade, something was growing. Alyssa bent to look at it. It was some kind of a woody fern. Plants weren't her specialty—she wanted to become a commercial artist, so her interests ran more to that side of life. But there was something odd about this plant, even granted it was growing in the middle of the desert. "Caitlin!" she yelled, and waited.

Her friend ambled over to join her. "What's up?" the redhead asked. "Lost the Charmin?"

Alyssa just pointed to the plant. "Know what that is?"

Caitlin joined her, her face furrowed in concentration. She was her father's daughter, and quite the A student. "It looks like a fern to me," she said, confused. "A woodland plant. What's it doing way out here in the desert? And how can it be surviving?"

"I don't know," Alyssa said. "Odd, isn't it?"

"Very," Caitlin agreed. "Still, it's nothing to concern us, really."

She couldn't have been more wrong, but at that time there was no way to know this . . .

CHAPTER 2

ONE OF THE biggest problems with the dig was that there was so little to do in their spare time. Alyssa had brought along her sketchbooks and water-colors, but there was something that bothered her about using watercolors to paint desert landscapes. It seemed to be so inappropriate. So she had stuck mostly to using colored pencils, and that bothered her, too. It seemed to be so much like being a child again. And, aside from the desert, there really wasn't much to paint.

Caitlin was suffering worse than Alyssa. Caitlin loved company, and her idea of heaven was dancing the night away in a club where you couldn't hear yourself breathing because of the ambient sound level of the band or deejay, and there was nothing like that here. The loudest noise in Furnace was the sound of the air conditioners trying to make indoors livable. And they didn't even have air conditioners in the tents.

This whole trip had been Caitlin's idea. She'd wanted to be a paleontologist forever, it seemed, just like her father. She'd had to beg and plead with him to be included on this dig, and then beg and plead some more to get Alyssa along, too. Normally assistants on these events had to be graduate students. Alyssa suspected that the only reason Dr. Weiss had caved in was that he didn't like the idea of paying for his daughter to be baby-sat all summer. The ex-Mrs. Weiss had announced that she'd done enough raising of children and had vanished off on a tour to some third world nation with her new steady, and left Dr. Weiss without anywhere else to place his daughter.

And Caitlin was obviously regretting her success. Oh, she loved the fieldwork. Kneeling in the dirt all day to wrestle a vertebra from the ground was just fine by her. It was the long, quiet nights that were wearing down her resolve. That was undoubtedly why she'd been flirting with Freeman earlier. He might be a wacko, but he was at least male and interesting.

The graduate students treated Caitlin with a mixture of polite contempt because of her age, and wary respect because of her father. Alyssa found most of them to be boring and elitist. The only exception was Donovan Leigh. He was English, over on some sort of transfer program, and he seemed more amused by the girls than annoyed. Caitlin had had a bad case of the Donovan Leighs. He was cute, had a lovely, exotic accent but, bummer!, a girlfriend back home to whom he was doggedly faithful. Caitlin was crushed. She had only reluctantly given up on him. It did not help matters either that Donovan seemed to pay more attention to Alyssa. He often hunted her down for "a chat" or to play Scrabble. And Alyssa secretly was flattered. After all, he really was *very* cute. But tonight she had something else on her mind. The fern she'd found earlier had inspired her to work. Something that wasn't orange or brown to paint! Something besides a rock! Snatching up her supplies and a folding stool, she headed off to find the plant.

Alyssa almost dropped her supplies. She could hardly believe her eyes! The plant was much bigger. Alyssa stared at it in disbelief. It was about four-feet tall and spreading out. Beside it was a woody growth that she couldn't place at all. And wisps of grass were appearing, too. She stared at the patch of greenery, confused. What was going on here? There hadn't been so much as a blade of grass all week, and now it was starting to look like they had their own oasis. Mentally shrugging, she set up the stool and easel, and started to sketch in her book. This stuff couldn't possibly last here, so she'd better take advantage of it while she could.

"Hello," said a British voice a short while later. "How's America's answer to John Constable today?"

"Happy to find a subject," Alyssa said, not turning around.

"A bunch of straggly plants?" Donovan asked. "Is that your idea of something to paint, then?"

"Unless you'd like me to paint you in the nude," she smirked. He laughed and rolled his eyes.

"Trust me, you don't need any more shocks in your life." He studied her sketch pad. "Actually, that's rather good."

"Thank you." She had started to dab in some color now, and was getting a feel for her subject. Only it wasn't quite right. . . . She'd somehow missed a small growth from the side of the fern. . . . She held her brush in her mouth while she sketched in the leaf she'd missed, and then continued her work. "I'm just glad to find something living in this desert that I don't need to hit with the heel of my shoe."

"Well thanks a lot," he said in an injured tone.

"Idiot." She couldn't help smiling. "I was referring to spiders."

"Oh," he said, sheepishly.

"By the way, how's Daisy?"

"Daphne," he corrected her, gently, for about the fortieth time. She was making a habit of getting his girl-friend's name wrong. "She's fine. And thanks for asking . . . Alice."

Alyssa nodded, and turned back to her work. That's funny, she thought. There was another leaf that she'd somehow missed. Maybe because Donovan was distracting her? Alyssa frowned. No, that wasn't it. She was a really good observer. Besides, there were now *two* woody growths next to the fern. "Donovan, how fast do ferns grow?"

"It's no good asking me, love," he replied. "I'm a city dweller. All this nature confuses me."

"I'm serious," she told him, leaning forward to examine the plant. "This has grown about four feet since this afternoon. And it's still putting out leaves. That can't be right."

"No," he agreed, more soberly. "Even I know that's not possible. I think we should go and have a word with Dr. West. She's into paleobotany, but I'm sure she'll know something about modern plants."

Alyssa nodded. She still wasn't entirely sure what all the specialist fields were in this dig, but she knew that Dr. West was probably the best person to consult. Maybe she was just overreacting, but there was something rather odd about this patch of fern. . . .

Bobby Marin was bored. He hated living in Furnace. His older brother and sister had hated it, too, till they had hit eighteen and moved out. Sensible, lucky folks. He had another two years to go. Why his mother hung around this dead town, he didn't know. Maybe it was because it was cheap, and she couldn't afford to move. There was certainly

TH E   I N V A D E R S   •

nothing much here to like. His only recreation was a battered VCR and a sixteen-inch TV. It could pick up some broadcast channels, just not too well. He was pretty much dependent on video tapes for amusement. And Chaney's store only had about three hundred to chose from. At two a night, that lasted him six months, tops. He pretty much knew them all backwards by now. The only video he hadn't watched was one with Pauly Shore. He cringed just thinking about it. Even he wasn't *that* hard up. Since the university crew had moved in just outside of town, digging up dinosaurs, Bobby had gone back to watching *Jurassic Park* over and over.

It was just fiction, he knew, but he enjoyed imagining what might happen if there was a park like that outside of town. It sure wouldn't be dull anymore! But he shut off the film partway through, stretched, and decided to take a walk. Twilight was on them, and that meant night in a few minutes. The heat would die down, and it would be tolerable outside. There wasn't much to do in town, of course, but maybe one of the girls from the university crew might come around. They wouldn't give a hick like him the time of day, of course, since he was so much younger than they were. But they were girls at least-girls from the city—and he could fantasize, if nothing else.

The night was still, and the ground radiated heat upward. His mom had tried to raise a few geraniums in pots on the stoop, but without much luck. Even they couldn't survive here. Bobby empathized with them, being forced to grow where they shouldn't even be. It was so much like his own life. Overhead, he could see the stars in a sprawl across the sky. He'd never bothered to learn the names of the constellations, except the Big Dipper. That was hard to miss. Still, they did look pretty.

He heard a dog howling, about half a mile away. Probably the Brewsters' old mutt. They left it roped up outdoors all the time. Maybe they thought it was a guard dog— though what did they have to guard, and against whom were they guarding it? But it got bored and just howled a lot. Bobby empathized with it, too. He felt like howling more often than not.

And then the howl changed to a whine, and then a yelp.

What the heck? Was somebody annoyed with its barking and throwing something at it?

Then it howled again, this time obviously in pain. Bobby felt his skin crawl, like he had bugs all over him. Something was wrong. . . .

He ran like crazy in the direction of the sound, wondering if someone was mistreating the old mutt. Bobby was no big animal lover, but hurting a dog seemed just plain wrong to him. He ran, and as he ran, he heard the whines getting shriller and shriller.

They cut off just before he reached the yard.

Dashing around the last corner, Bobby skidded to a halt, staring in shock into the Brewster's yard. The old mutt had been silenced, all right. Its throat had been torn out and there was blood pooled and spattered all over the dirt. There was no sign of the Brewsters. Probably down in Chaney's store, Bobby figured, like most of the adults, drinking and gossiping, the jukebox playing loud to drown out reality.

Who could have done this to the old dog? Or what? A coyote, maybe. But he hadn't heard of any coyotes hanging around. And there wasn't much else big enough to take on a hound dog, even an old one.

''What the—'' Suddenly something dashed out of the yard. Bobby didn't get a good look at it, considering it was pretty dark. But whatever it was, it was moving pretty fast and hugging the ground.

It was an animal. Bobby was certain of that. It ran on

two legs, its long head held low, its jaws stained with blood. Also, it was big. It looked to be about six feet long, and sleek.

It was also a dark color, scaled and fanged.

Bobby felt his blood running as cold as ice.

It was gone in a second, swallowed up by desert shadows. All Bobby could hear was the drumming of the starlight and the paniced hammering of his own heart. *Could* he have seen what he saw? It made no sense. But he was convinced of one thing:

It had looked just like one of those raptors from *Jurassic Park*.

A *dinosaur. . . .*

CHAPTER 3

ALYSSA HAD BEEN curious enough about the ferns to seek out Dr. West for an explanation. The truth was, the whole fern business was giving Alyssa the creeps. Dr. West, too, had been puzzled and had taken samples back to camp to investigate. Alyssa had hoped Dr. West could reassure her. But all Dr. West had concluded was what Alyssa already knew: the growth was abnormal.

Something was wrong. Alyssa knew it. That morning she headed over to use the tent, and stopped in her tracks.

There were now two small trees, several shoots, and a patch of ferns about ten feet across. All in the course of one day, in the desert.

It made no kind of rational sense that Alyssa could see. Caitlin, on the other hand, wasn't at all bothered.

"It happens," she told her friend. "Seeds and spores can lay dormant in the desert for months or even years. All they need is water, and then they spring back to life. It looks odd, but it's not unusual.''

"Where did the water come from, then?" asked Alyssa, unconvinced.

"The toilet, the showers . . . Us, in general," Caitlin replied, shrugging. "Life will find a way. They don't need that much water to set them growing."

Alyssa still didn't buy this explanation. "If they're getting the water from our use, then why aren't they growing next to the shower tent or toilet tent, and not out there?"

"Maybe that's where the toilet tent was last," Caitlin answered, irritation creeping into her voice. "And it took a week or so for the growth to kick in. How should I know? Alyssa, I think the heat's getting to you. Why are you trying to make a mystery out of something so simple?"

"Because I don't think it is simple," Alyssa said honestly. "It's creepy."

"This whole desert is creepy," Caitlin answered. "That's minor stuff, as far as I'm concerned."

Maybe Caitlin was right, shrugged Alyssa. But it bothered her, just the same. It all seemed to be so *wrong*. She wanted to talk more with Dr. West about it. Alyssa found her already hard at work in her tent. Dr. West was wrapping plaster-soaked bandages about the excavated bones, strengthening them for the return to the campus laboratory. Alyssa knew better than to disturb Dr. West, whose temper was legendary. Later, Alyssa thought. Alyssa went back to work with Caitlin on gently digging up the vertebra of a *Baryonyx*. But her mind was still focused on the plants. At around the mid morning break Alyssa noticed a funnel of dust being kicked up in the desert toward town. Caitlin jumped to attention. "Think it might be Freeman?" she asked.

Figures, thought Alyssa. But she shook her head.

"Wrong direction," Alyssa said. Caitlin looked crushed. Not wanting to disappoint her friend, Alyssa added: "Unless he's been to town first."

It was the sheriff, instead. He drew to a halt just outside of camp, and walked easily over to the table where Caitlin's father was working.

"Morning, Professor," he said amiably. Dr. Weiss sighed irritably. He had given up trying to explain to the sheriff the difference between a *professor*—which he wasn't—and a *doctor*—which he was. "Wonder if you might be able to spare some time to come into town?"

Dr. Weiss looked impatiently towards the excavation site. Donovan and two of the others were in the last stages of freeing a femur, an extremely delicate maneuver. "I'm rather busy right now," he replied. "Is it important?"

"Probably not," admitted the sheriff. "More than likely it's just local trouble. Dog got killed last night. Young Bobby Marin was found near the dog, and he's telling the wildest story I ever heard. Says a dinosaur killed the dog."

"A *dinosaur*?" Dr. Weiss laughed. "Honestly, Sheriff, I know that the locals aren't exactly the brightest folks in the country, but surely even they know dinosaurs died out millions of years ago?"

Alyssa thought that this remark was definitely on the insulting side, but the sheriff didn't seem to be too offended. "Yeah, we heard something like that. And Bobby has been watching that dinosaur movie. My guess is he most likely killed the dog himself and is trying to make up a story to get off the hook."

Dr. Weiss arched his eyebrows patronizingly. "Then I don't see any need for me to be bothered, Sheriff. Do you?" Then he gave the sheriff an impatient look. "Surely you can deal with that?"

"That I can," agreed Sheriff Gates. "It's the tracks I got problems with."

"Tracks?"

The Sheriff nodded. "Looks like a big chicken ran through the area. A six-foot chicken. Of course, we know there aren't any six-foot chickens, either. I'd just like an expert to take a peek and give me an intelligent opinion."

Dr. Weiss sighed. "I can't spare the time right now. Perhaps Dr. West might be able to help. She's good at taking plaster casts."

Alyssa saw her chance to get away from the dig for a while. "I'll get her," she offered quickly, and then headed for the doctor's tent. Dr. West was still working on wrapping specimens. Alyssa explained the sheriff's request, and Dr. West frowned.

"Trust Sam to volunteer me for the job. Oh, well . . . It'll be good for community relations."

"I'd be happy to come along and give you a hand," Alyssa offered.

"That's kind of you," Dr. West said happily. "If they want me to take plaster casts, I could do with an assistant. Can you get me a sack of the plaster ready while I wash up?" She held up her own plaster-encrusted hands. "I'll just be a moment."

Ten minutes later, the two of them were in the sheriff's patrol car with the plaster and forms in the trunk. The sheriff had his air conditioning full on, and Alyssa felt happy again. It was only a short break from the monotony of the excavation, but she'd take whatever she could.

"You realize that there can't possibly be anything to this boy's story, Sheriff?" Dr. West said.

"Naturally, ma'am," Gates agreed. "But it's my job to check everything, no matter how crazy it sounds."

Dr. West smiled. "Mine, too. Only the bodies I investigate are a little older than yours."

The sheriff grinned back, obviously a lot more comfortable with Dr. West than with Dr. Weiss. Alyssa couldn't blame him; she preferred Dr. West, too.

It didn't take long to reach the town, and then the sheriff pulled his car up outside the Brewster house. Like most of the homes in Furnace, it was slightly seedy, and with a yard that was more parched dirt than grass. There was a doghouse and a large bowl of water in the back. Alyssa noticed a dark stain on the ground. She also noticed a strange cross-hatching of freshly clawed runnels in the dirt.

"Where's the dog?" asked Dr. West. She knelt down to examine the ground.

"I had it removed," the sheriff explained. "Didn't think you'd need to see it."

"Probably not," agreed Dr. West. "What about these marks?"

"There's more." He pointed, then led the way to the far side of the yard. "The ground here's a bit too baked to allow prints, but Mrs. Brewster's been trying to raise tomatoes, and she did some watering." The garden was pockmarked with a stand of withered tomato plants." He showed them that many of the vines had been snapped off, almost as if with a knife.

"It could have been another dog or a coyote," concluded Dr. West.

The sheriff blew out his checks. "That's what I figured. But look at this."

In the softer mud was a footprint, and a second.

Dr. West's eyes widened. "Obviously some kind of three-toed creature," she judged. "With claws. These prints are almost a foot long!"

"Like I said, it would have taken a monster chicken to make marks like this."

Dr. West's eyes narrowed. "Odd," she decided. "Some sort of bipedal creature, sure enough. Must have stood at least six feet tall, judging from the spacing between the prints. Hard to estimate the weight of it without knowing how hard the ground is, but I'd say that there was definitely some kind of animal here last night, Sheriff. Running, too— the weight's on the front of the foot." She turned. "Alyssa, please get me my equipment. I definitely want a cast of these prints."

Alyssa fetched the plaster, bucket, and the wooden former. Dr. West placed this around the print, and then glanced at the sheriff. "Can I get some water to mix up the plaster?"

"I'll go ask Mrs. Brewster," the Sheriff said. "She's taking the loss of her dog kind of hard."

Despite the ferocious heat, Alyssa again felt a chill run down her spine. The dog was obviously left outside almost all the time. She could see the post to which it was normally chained, close to the doghouse. And the large water dish indicated that it was filled infrequently. The animal had been a guard dog. A very *large* guard dog from the looks of it. What could have attacked it, then, and killed it? She didn't know of many animals that would take on a dog.

Mrs. Brewster came out with a large pitcher of water, which she handed wordlessly to Dr. West. The Doctor mixed up the plaster and poured it into the mold. Mrs. Brewster—a tall, thin, dried-up looking woman—turned to Sheriff Gates. "You arrested that hoodlum Bobby Marin yet?" she demanded. "I don't know what all this foolishness is about. He's the one who must have done it."

"We don't know that for certain, Mrs. Brewster," the

sheriff replied politely. "I'm duty bound to check all possibilities."

"You do that, Sheriff," the woman agreed. "Then you arrest that Bobby. He's a bad kid. A malcontent."

Can't blame him, if he lives in this town, thought Alyssa. She glanced at the tomato plants while Dr. West prepared the plaster casts. Then she stiffened.

Ferns had sprouted among the tomato plants, ferns that looked identical to the ones out at the dig.

"Excuse me, Mrs. Brewster," she said politely. "Those ferns—are they a local plant?"

"Ferns?" the woman asked blankly. Then she saw what Alyssa meant. "Heavens! Weeds! How is it that a body can't get tomatoes to grow, but weeds spring up overnight?" She bent to pull them out.

"Overnight?" Alyssa asked. "You mean they weren't there yesterday?"

"They certainly were not," Mrs. Brewster replied, yanking out a handful of them. "I keep a tidy garden."

It had to be a coincidence, but Alyssa couldn't help wondering. Ferns growing out in the camp where nothing else would grow. Now ferns here where tomatoes wouldn't grow. She turned to Dr. West. "Do you need me for the next ten minutes?" she asked. "I'd just like to head into town to check into something."

Dr. West grinned. "Sure, Alyssa. Just don't take too long about it. I'll need you to help me once these casts are dry."

Alyssa hurried off. A wild idea had occurred to her, and she needed some kind of proof. . . .

She stopped at the second house on the main street just past the only video store. There was a woman seated in a rocker on the porch, drinking cold lemonade. Next to her was a row of pots, each containing a couple of ferns.

"Excuse me," Alyssa said politely. "Can you tell me what kind of a fern that is?"

"Fern?" The woman looked down at the pots and scowled. "Those are my geranium pots!" She looked confused, then incensed. "You aren't one of them high school punks, are you? This your idea of a sick joke?"

Alyssa rolled her eyes, and sighed.

"No," Alyssa explained patiently. "I just got into town with the sheriff. This is as close to your pots as I've ever been."

"Well," huffed the old woman. "Who would do a foolish thing like that?" Alyssa said she didn't know, then waved goodbye.

"Hoodlums," muttered the old woman. "Nothin' but a bunch of juvenile delinquents!"

Alyssa sighed. "Whatever."

There were fourteen more ferns growing in pots all over town. In no case did the owners know how they had managed to get there. Alyssa finished her survey at Chaney's General Store. She asked Mr. Chaney if he sold plants.

"Sure do," he confirmed. "Some nice, hardy stock. You're from that dinosaur group, right? Looking to brighten up the place a bit?"

"Something like that," Alyssa agreed vaguely. She accompanied him to the small greenhouse behind the store. Unlike Mr. Chaney, she wasn't too surprised at what he found there.

"Well, how did *that* happen?" he demanded, removing his baseball cap to scratch at his bald head. All of his flowers were gone. In their place had blossomed the inevitable ferns.

"I don't know," Alyssa said truthfully. She went back to the Brewster home deep in thought. *Something* was making those ferns grow all over the place in town, as well as out at the dig. And yet nowhere else in the area. Why ferns? And what could possibly be doing this? It was peculiar, to say the least, and Alyssa was starting to get scared.

Back at the Brewster place Dr. West was gently prying the dried plaster from the prints when Alyssa returned. "Ah!" Dr. West called out. "Just in time."

Alyssa glanced at the tomato plants. In the ground where Mrs. Brewster had ripped out the ferns, a new crop of seedlings was already sprouting.

"Alyssa!" called Dr. West. The young girl blinked awake, as if from a trance. "Are you alright?"

Alyssa nodded. "Fine."

"Good. Come here, then. I thought you might want to take a look at this." Dr. West turned the plaster cast upside down. It showed a perfectly clear portion of a three-toed foot, two forward, one backward. Claws were very obvious, as was the ridging of scales on the toes.

"Well, ma'am?" Sheriff Gates asked the doctor. "What made them tracks? They look like some big bird."

"It could be a large bird," Dr. West confirmed. "Maybe an ostrich, though I'm not really too sure of that. I'd have to check. There's no ostrich farms around here, are there?"

"No, ma'am," the sheriff answered. "Be kind of hard to overlook if there were. Is there anything else it could be?"

Dr. West sighed. "If it wasn't impossible, Sheriff," she confessed, "I'd say that there was a possibility that it *was* a dinosaur. It has every indication of being from that group. But, of course, it couldn't be."

"No, ma'am," the sheriff agreed. "Well, let's get that into the evidence locker, and I'm going to have to have a long, hard think about what I'm going to do about this case. It sure does beat all."

"You can say that again," Dr. West agreed. "You can

pack this equipment away again now," she told Alyssa. "Did you find what you were after in town?"

"Yes," Alyssa said, lugging the the plaster to the patrol car. "Only I don't know what to make of it." She gestured at the tomatoes. "Look what's growing there."

Dr. West bent to look, and then frowned again. "More ferns?"

"They're all over town," Alyssa informed her. "The neighbors think that somebody's been stealing their plants and putting ferns in their place as some sort of grand practical joke."

"It seems rather pointless to me," Dr. West commented.

"As well as very hard to do," Alyssa agreed. "Besides, where would the joker get the ferns from in the first place? And why are they thriving when everything else around here is dying?"

"I don't know," Dr. West said slowly. She shook her head. "There's something very odd going on in this town, Alyssa. I can't identify those ferns in any of my texts. I've tried to do a search of the university data bank via the internet, to see if I can discover anything that way. But it's very peculiar."

"And this story about a dinosaur killing the dog?" Alyssa asked her.

"Not very logical, is it, Alyssa?" Dr. West said quietly. "You know that the dinosaurs died out sixty million years ago. There can't possibly be one left alive today."

"Then what made those tracks?" Alyssa asked. "Do you really think it was an ostrich, or something?"

Dr. West shrugged. "What other logical possibility is there?"

"I don't know," Alyssa admitted. And that was what bothered her. . . .

CHAPTER 4

WHEN THEY RETURNED to the camp, Alyssa saw the militia's humvee and realized that Denby was back.

"Uh oh," she warned Dr. West. "Looks like trouble."

Caitlin met the sheriff's car, her face glum.

"Denby's ranting and raving," she told them. "He seems to think Dad's trying to get him into trouble with the FBI, the CIA and even the FCC. Sheriff, you've got to go talk to him!"

Sheriff Gates sighed. "That man is more trouble than a skunk down your trousers," he muttered. "Okay, I'll go see what I can do." He ambled off, and Caitlin turned to Alyssa.

"And he didn't even bring Freeman this time," she complained. "Bummer. So, how did the great dinosaur hunt go?"

Alyssa shrugged. "We found *something*," she said, helping to remove Dr. West's stuff from the patrol car. "Give me a hand with this, will you?" Together, the two girls took the supplies back to the doctor's tent.

"Damnation!" Dr. West exclaimed, staring at her specimen table. "It's got to be that stupid man!"

Alyssa stared at the table, and saw that two more of the eggs had been shattered. Shards of stone were scattered everywhere. There were only three eggs left intact.

"I'm going to set the sheriff on him this time for sure," Dr. West snapped, marching out of the tent.

"Boy, the trouble never ends, does it?" Caitlin asked, looking slightly amused. "It must be the heat, frying everyone's brains."

"You're assuming they all had brains to begin with," Alyssa answered. "And I'm not at all convinced Denby did." She examined the shattered specimens. "Caitlin, look at this. Notice something odd?"

Caitlin bent to examine the pieces that Alyssa had pointed out. "They look like they've been hit with a mallet. Nobody in our team would even dream of doing something like that. Dr. West's right, it's got to be those stupid survivalists."

"No, that's not what I mean." Alyssa picked up one of the larger pieces. "Look at this. It's convex on the outside, which is right, since the eggs are spheres. And it's concave on the inside."

"So, it's . . ." Caitlin's voice trailed off as she suddenly saw what her friend meant. "These eggs are *hollow*?"

"They must be," Alyssa said. "I'll bet if we reassembled them, all three of the broken eggs would be hollow."

Caitlin had paled. She shook her head firmly. "That's impossible. Dinosaur eggs are *never* hollow. The fetus inside and the amniotic fluid all fossilize, along with the egg. Dinosaur eggs are always solid."

"*These* aren't." Alyssa realized what she was about to suggest sounded dumb, but she said it anyway. "What if they really *are* eggs somehow? And whatever was inside them survived?"

Caitlin gave her an incredulous look. "Stick to your sketchbooks, Alyssa. You'd make a lousy scientist. These things have been buried for sixty million years. *Nothing* could live for that length of time."

"I know," said Alyssa. She even sounded dumb to herself. But she pressed on. "I remember reading that scientists had discovered some perfectly preserved wheat seeds in one of the pyramids. And when they planted them, they grew."

"Alyssa!" Caitlin laughed. "The pyramids are only a few thousand years old, not millions! And wheat seeds are a lot different to live dinosaurs! Get a grip. You've been out in the sun too long."

"Maybe I have," Alyssa agreed, tired suddenly. "But there's something really spooky going on here. Those weird ferns out there all over town now, too."

"So?" Caitlin obviously didn't see anything odd in this.

"They weren't there yesterday," Alyssa answered. "And last night a kid saw a dinosaur attack a dog."

"A kid *claims* he saw a dinosaur," Caitlin replied. "Did anyone else see it?"

"There aren't many people out and about in Furnace," Alyssa answered.

"I thought not." Caitlin took Alyssa's hand. "Look, I know you're not really having much fun here, and I'm sorry. But there's no need to start making up mysteries and stories where none exist."

The tent flap opened, and Dr. West came in. "That man's impossible," she snapped.

Alyssa raised an eyebrow. "Which man?" As far as

Alyssa could tell, it was a description that applied equally
to Dr. Weiss *or* Denby.

"Denby," Dr. West answered. "He's accusing us of faking the dinosaur sighting in town as a pretext for bringing
in government reinforcements. He believes our real target
is his militia. He thinks Dr. Weiss is really a military com-
mander and we are just decoys to deflect suspicion. That
man is seriously delusional."

"I'll bet he denies having broken the eggs, too," Alyssa
suggested.

"Of course he does!" The doctor slapped her hand down
on the nearest table, rattling bones. "But who else could
have done it?"

"I don't think it's a *who*," Alyssa ventured. Dr. West
and Caitlin looked at her sharply. "Take a look at the fragments. They're hollow."

"*Hollow?*" repeated Dr. West. "No. That can't be right.
She examined the fragments. "You're right, Alyssa—they
are hollow." She stared from the fragments to the intact
eggs and back. "And more than that . . . Get me the glue,
will you?" She started sorting through the pieces, pulling
out the largest. Alyssa handed her the adhesive, and the
doctor started to patch portions of the shell back together.

There were lots of gaps, but the chunks fit together pretty
clearly back into an egg shape. Holding it gently in her
hand, Dr. West lifted one of the intact eggs up in her right
hand. "The intact egg's at least three times heavier," she
commented. "And look at the size." Alyssa studied them;
the broken egg was only about four inches across, while
the intact one was about six. "They were all this size last
night," Dr. West said softly.

"Then where has the rest of the stone gone to?" Caitlin
demanded. "It didn't just evaporate."

"No," agreed Dr. West thoughtfully. "But *something*

happened to it. I wonder what?'' She placed the repaired egg down on the table. ''I think I'd better lock these last three eggs away somewhere safe.'' She crossed to the large trestle table where she had most of her equipment hooked up. They'd run a power line into the tent from a small generator for the equipment, and a telephone line in from the town for the internet connection. ''It figures,'' Dr. West said with a sigh. ''The computer's down, too. You get lousy service in this flea-infested town.''

This was getting more confusing by the minute. Alyssa couldn't make any sense out of this whole affair. And it was quite clear that, whatever was happening here, it was way out of Dr. West's league, too.

Which wasn't very encouraging.

Freeman was worried. Normally, he'd have been as pleased as anything to be sent on a special mission, but this one bothered him. Not that he was questioning the colonel's orders, of course. It was just . . . well, that this was targeted against the scientists at the excavation. And, by implication, those two pretty girls, too.

He didn't quite know what to make of those girls. They had been brainwashed by the government, of course, but that didn't really make them his enemies. Just ignorant. They didn't see that there was a war was being waged between the government and the people. The government wanted to rob the people of their rights as guaranteed under the Constitution. They were using the courts, the FBI and all the rest to chip away at personal freedoms and liberties. But they were doing it slowly, and quietly, so that no one would hardly notice. That was so obvious. But girls like those two, they were encouraged to waste time thinking about other things, like boys, and dating, and shopping at the mall. Not to think for themselves, but to think as they were told to think.

Still, they seemed pretty bright to Freeman. Maybe he could explain how things really stood if he had a chance.

But the colonel had ruled that out when Freeman had suggested that he be allowed to go visit the camp. "They get their funding from the government," Colonel Denby had pointed out. "The government controls them. There's a covert military agent in that camp. They're staging an assault on us. But they're tricky. They know they can't attack us head on. So they're camaflouging their motives, pretending to be scientists. You're a good boy, Freeman. You don't want to get mixed up with folks like that and all their lies."

That was the problem, though: he *did* want to get mixed up with at least two of them. There weren't any kids his age in the militia, and *no* girls. And Alyssa and Caitlin were so good-looking and friendly . . . But orders were orders, and he couldn't disobey, though he was at least slightly tempted to do so right now.

Freeman and Quinlan had been sent out west of town to where the telephone wires had been hung.

"They've got a computer in their camp," the colonel had explained. "It's hooked into that internet thing, which is a tool the repressive government uses to disseminate information about us. They're no doubt reporting back to Washington all about us right now. We may have to expect a raid any time now. Freeman, you and Quinlan go out there and cut those lines. Get them off that internet, and do it *now*."

So Quinlan was up the pole. He'd worked for the phone company once, before he'd wised up to the fact that they were just the tool of the government. Of course, he didn't know exactly which line the computer had accessed, so he'd been forced to start cutting them all to make certain he got the right one. It was the first rule of any combat operation. Seize and control the lines of communication. It made perfect sense. The Colonel had said so.

Freeman sighed. Everything made sense. Except why he had to fight against those two girls. He didn't like the way that made him feel. Maybe the adults in the camp were dupes or spies, but not the girls. It felt wrong to him to be going up against them like this.

Shielding his eyes against the glare of the sun, he stared up at Quinlan on the pole. "You going to be much longer, Quin?"

"Soon be done," Quinlan called back. "Just another two to go, and we can be out of here."

"This going to stop them for long?" Freeman asked.

"Hard to say. They're bound to notice the break soon, and then they'll have to go outside town for help. I figure this will last two, three days at most."

"And then what?"

Quinlan grunted. "That's the colonel's place to say," he answered. "Okay, starting on the last one now."

Freeman wasn't satisfied, but he shut up. There wasn't much else he could do. Then there came a commotion from the humvee, and Horse started to howl. "What the blazes!" Freeman sprinted back to the vehicle. Horse was in the backseat, whining and howling, pawing at the window in a frenzy. Freeman had never seen him act like this unless there was trouble. "What is it, boy?" he demanded, opening the door.

Horse leaped through the open door, sending Freeman sprawling to the ground. Freeman's head smacked hard against the dry earth. It was like concrete, and the pain made his senses reel. Damned dog, he groaned. Probably caught a whiff of gopher or something. . . .

There was a dark shadow overhead. Horse was barking and yowling. Freeman tried to get up, but his head wasn't working straight. He couldn't quite get his mind focused.

Then Quinlan screamed.

Then, just as abruptly, he stopped screaming.

Horse was still going wild, trying to leap up the pole after something. Freeman realized something very wrong was happening. He struggled to his elbow, and managed to stare up the pole. His eyes weren't working right, but he could see a huge, shadowy *something* attacking Quinlan.

Freeman fumbled for his pistol, and managed to pull it free on the third attempt. His vision was blurred as he tried to aim at whatever was up there. But his hand shook too much. Damn that dog for this! Freeman slid back to the humvee, resting his back against the huge tire, and then used both hands to raise the gun. He squeezed off two shaky shots.

The shadow shrieked, and then beat large, leathery wings. Freeman could make out a long beak, which had been ripping at Quinlan's body. The bird spread its wings, and flapped like crazy. Horse was almost foaming at the mouth, trying to get up the pole to tear the thing apart. Freeman managed another shot. The thing squalled again, and then flapped hard, flying away.

Freeman staggered to his feet, and flung open the humvee door. There was a container of water inside, and he used it to dowse his head. Shaking his hair dry, he straightened up. He could focus his eyes now, and his head didn't feel like it was going to explode any second. He stood firm, and turned to see what had happened.

Quinlan's body was tangled in the wires at the top of the pole. "Quin!" Freeman yelled. He called out again. "Quin!"

The body twisted in the breeze, and Freeman saw Quin's face. It had been nearly torn free. And his chest and stomach looked like it had been opened up with a jack hammer. Freeman bent over and threw up his breakfast.

"Oh my God," he moaned. He heaved again.

Freeman used the water to rinse his mouth out, and then sat down, not daring to look up the pole. Quinlan was dead. He could hear Horse whimpering behind him. What was he going to do about him? The thought of climbing up and trying to figure out a way of lowering the body made him shake again. There was no way he was going to do that. He'd have to go and get help. That meant back to the farm, where the rest of the militia was.

Would it be okay to just leave Quinlan up there like that? Or would that thing come back to finish its meal? Heck, there wasn't much that Freeman could do about that. He'd have to go for help on this one. If that giant bird came back, well, Quin was past feeling anything now. Calling Horse to the humvee, Freeman jumped in the front seat and drove away as fast as he dared.

What kind of bird would attack a man like that? he wondered dazedly. He'd never heard of anything like it. Maybe the colonel was right, and the government was starting their attack. The "bird" he saw might have been some new, top secret weapon. Maybe Quin was just the first victim in the war. After all, who knew what kind of weapons the crazies in the government had by now? Freeman knew they were into genetic engineering, breeding fake sheep and all that. What if they'd also bred a killer bird, just to take out the loyalist militia? The colonel had to know about this attack as soon as possible.

And he'd then know what to do about it. . . .

CHAPTER 5

ALYSSA STARED AT the patch of ferns with growing alarm. Actually, "patch" was no longer the word for it—there was almost an acre of forest-level growth there now. Luckily, it seemed to be spreading away from camp, but it was still very unsettling. "You want to try telling me that you think *that's* normal?" she demanded of Caitlin.

Her friend scratched at the back of her neck, where she'd started to peel a little from the sun. "It is a bit extreme," she admitted.

"A *bit*?" Alyssa gestured at the stand. "There are small pine trees and roses in there, for heaven's sake! How would they grow in a desert?"

"Well, they *are* growing," Caitlin said stubbornly. "There's got to be a perfectly rational explanation for what's happening there."

"Of course there has," Alyssa agreed. "But I haven't

heard anybody come up with one yet. Your father seems to be treating this forest like it doesn't exist, and Dr. West is too bothered about her fossil eggs to pay any attention to this.''

"Then let's take a look," Caitlin suggested. "Digging's over for the day, and we're not on cooking duty, so we can mess about in there for a while. Let's see what's going on.''

Alyssa didn't like the idea of them venturing out there alone, but she could hardly object without looking like a wimp. Something about the plants terrified her. And it wasn't just the fact that they were growing so fast. It was something else. Where did the plants come from? And *why*?

Caitlin plunged into the undergrowth, grinning happily as she stirred up a cloud of small insects. "Boy, it's a regular little ecology in here. Where did all of these bugs come from?''

"I don't know," Alyssa answered. "Maybe you'd better watch out for scorpions or snakes, Cait.''

"You're *really* getting a mother-hen complex, aren't you?" Caitlin asked. "I'm a big girl now, and I'm not going to do anything stupid.''

Coming in here could probably be classified as stupid, Alyssa thought. But there was no point in saying that aloud. She watched the ground and the plants with equal concern. She only had sandals on her feet, and her legs were totally unprotected. There were small climbing roses in here that could scratch her badly if she stumbled into them. And who knew what kind of other life?

"Magnolias," Caitlin breathed. "This is astonishing.'' She was enraptured by a small bush.

"This is scary," Alyssa confessed. "None of this should be here.''

"So what do you want to do?" Caitlin asked. "Deport

it? Alyssa, I don't understand you. You're not normally this nervous. What's gotten into you?''

"This place is *wrong*," Alyssa insisted. "It shouldn't be here, and it should be dying anyway. Instead, it's growing like crazy. If that doesn't worry you, I don't know what else to say. It's unnatural.''

"Look, I understand what you're saying," her friend answered. "But I think you're making too big a deal out of nothing. After all, mother nature is nothing if not mysterious." She gave a peal of laughter as a huge dragonfly buzzed across between two bushes. "Isn't this great?''

"It's not the word I'd use." Alyssa watched the dragonfly darting about. "Aren't those things normally found near water?''

That made Caitlin pause a moment. "Yes," she agreed, puzzled. "They are. But there's not enough here for it, is there?''

"Not unless a lake's sprung up, too," Alyssa replied. "Cait, this place is getting really bizarre.''

The dragonfly shot off between two rose vines. Caitlin plunged headlong after it. "Let's see where it's getting its water," she called back.

Sighing, Alyssa followed the other girl, but with considerably less abandon. Who knew what might be lurking in the shadows in here? There was just so much growing. Alyssa had a sudden vision of the patch expanding so fast that the two of them would never be able to get out of it again. She forced that image from her mind, and tried to concentrate on the task at hand.

The plants and small trees abruptly stopped, and so did Caitlin. Alyssa peered over her friend's shoulder and couldn't repress a chill.

There was a small pond ahead of them, about eight feet across.

And there definitely hadn't been anything of the kind the previous day. Since there had been no rain, and this was in the middle of the desert, where had the water come from?

"You know," Caitlin said, "I'm starting to think you may be right about this place. This is impossible."

"Yes." Alyssa stared at the pond, and then moved closer to peer into it. "Cait, there are *fish* in here!"

"Huh?" The other girl knelt to look. "Jeez, this really is creepy. I could maybe understand how plant spores lying dormant in the soil could suddenly revive, but *fish*? No way.

"Aren't there some fish that can bury themselves in mud and survive periods of drought?" asked Alyssa.

"This is a *desert,* not mud," Caitlin answered. "There's not been water here in . . . oh, thousands, maybe millions of years."

"Millions of years?" Alyssa echoed. "Like sixty million perhaps?"

Caitlin gave her a pained look. "Don't start with that nonsense again. *Nothing* could survive sixty million years in hibernation. Not fish, not dinosaurs."

Alyssa nodded slowly. "I guess you're right. It is pretty silly. Besides, we saw roses and magnolias, didn't we? I thought flowering plants evolved after dinosaurs."

That made Caitlin pause. "Actually," she said in a low voice, "they didn't." She looked around the clearing. "All of the plants here had evolved by the Cretaceous period. The Earth would have looked something like this when the dinosaurs were alive. But that doesn't mean anything."

Alyssa wasn't so sure. She had to agree, there didn't seem to be any way for something to have hatched out of those broken spheres. "*Nothing* could live sixty million years in hibernation right?" she asked. "Right?"

"Nothing," Caitlin said flatly. "Not even viruses. They've been known to go dormant for long periods of time and then revitalize. But nothing along those kind of lines. Besides," she waved her hand about, "this is considerably more advanced life than a virus."

"You're right," agreed Alyssa. When it came to paleontology, Caitlin was the expert.

Caitlin glanced into the pond again, watching the darting fish. They were all quite small, but active. "Let's catch one," she suggested. "We could have Dr. West look at it."

"I don't think that's such"—Alyssa began, but too late. Caitlin plunged both hands into the pond, trying to grab one of the fish. It darted away, and she chased after it, leaning out over the water.

Then she gave a yelp of pain, and pulled her hand out. A tiny fish was attached to the flat of Caitlin's palm. It thrashed about wildly, then let go, leaving a pinprick trail of blood.

Caitlin stared at her hand uncomprehendingly.

"Caitlin," Alyssa asked, "are you okay?"

Alyssa hadn't caught more than a glimpse of it, but it had looked very wrong. Instead of scales, it seemed to have armored segments, almost like an insect, rather than a fish.

"Damn!" Caitlin swore, putting her hand to her mouth and sucking at the wound. "Stupid thing *bit* me. But, yeah. I'm okay."

"I knew you shouldn't have done that," Alyssa said.

"You're very smart all of a sudden," Caitlin snapped. Then she softened. "I'm sorry, Alyssa. I didn't mean that."

"It's alright," Alyssa assured her. Caitlin's temper sometimes got the better of her. She always blamed it on her red hair, but Alyssa suspected it was due to tensions at home. Her father and mother hadn't managed to have a stable marriage, and there had always been a lot of anger in the house. Some of it had naturally rubbed off on Caitlin. "Maybe we should get back and put some disinfectant or something on the bite."

"It's not that bad, really," Caitlin insisted, clambering back to her feet. She held her hand out for Alyssa's inspection. "It's almost stopped bleeding already, look."

Alyssa took Caitlin's hand and examined the wound. There were about a dozen needle–sized puncture marks, but Caitlin was right. The bleeding was almost halted. She managed a grin. "You going to tell everyone about the one that got away?" she asked.

Caitlin laughed. "Only if you promise to swear it was at least three feet long. You're right, though, we'd better get back. It must almost be time for dinner." She glared at the pond. "I really hope it's fish. I'd like to bite one back."

Freeman was standing to attention, back at the base of the telephone pole. He watched from the corner of his eye as the colonel and two of the other men managed to maneuver Quinlan's body—or what was left of it—into a body bag. He winced as he heard the sound of the zipper. He'd never seen a man die before, and he had never imagined it looking and smelling this bad. The only way he could avoid throwing up again was to focus on standing to attention, and waiting for the others to come down again.

"Heads up below," Carter called, and Freeman looked up. They had a rope attached to the body bag now. "Grab hold of this and lower him steady to the ground."

Freeman didn't like the thought of touching the bag, but he knew what his duty was. As they lowered down the bag, he caught it and guided it gently to the ground. Enough had happened to Quin already; he didn't need to be treated like a sack of potatoes. Then the three men up the pole all came down. Freeman noticed that the colonel was the last, and he'd had his AK-47 cradled in his arms the whole time they were up the pole.

As Carter and Semanski loaded the body into the truck, Colonel Denby came over to where Freeman stood. "At ease, soldier," the colonel said. He nodded at the body bag. "You say a bird did that to him?"

"I'm not certain, sir," Freeman admitted. "I'd banged my head, and couldn't see quite straight. But it sure was something with wings, and I don't see what else it could have been, sir."

"Nor me, either," the colonel admitted. "But I've never heard of a bird that would attack a grown, healthy man and do that kind of damage to him." He rubbed his chin. "It makes me think that the government's up to something." He gave Freeman a cold stare. "You ever seen that *Jurassic Park* movie, son?"

"No, sir." Freeman was puzzled, because the colonel didn't approve of watching movies. Like the telephone company, the motion picture industry was just another government tool. "An instrument of party propaganda," the colonel called it.

"Me neither," the colonel admitted. "But I understand it was all about a secret program to bring the dinosaurs back to life . . ." He stared thoughtfully into the desert. "And we've got ourselves a whole bunch of those government-funded scientists out there, digging up bits of dinosaur bones. Do you believe that they're just after them things so they can put them on display in a museum?"

Freeman was getting lost here. "But . . . Why else would they be digging them up, sir?"

"You ever been to a museum?" the colonel asked. "If you had, you'd have known that most of the so-called dinosaurs on display there aren't the real things at all. They're *copies*. So, what happened to the originals, hey?" He stared into the desert again. "Maybe that movie was deliberate propaganda. I've been thinking that maybe the government's been working on bringing back dinosaurs, and they had the film made to prepare the people for just such a thing." He looked reflective. "I was talking to Sheriff Gates. Now, it's true enough he's employed by the Powers That Be, but he ain't a bad man. Not yet, anyway. He tells me that a kid spotted a real-live dinosaur in town last night. Attacked and half-ate a dog. And now some damned bird comes flying in, attacks and half-eats one of us. I may be a lot of things, boy, but I'm not stupid. You don't need to hit me with a two-by-four to get my attention."

"Sir?" Freeman asked, hopelessly confused.

"I think those scientists out there in the desert are working on bringing back the dinosaurs, Freeman," the colonel said firmly. "They're using what they dig up to make new ones. Hell, they've even got some eggs, and maybe some high-tech way of hatching them things out. That's why they got so upset when those eggs got busted up. Either way, they've got themselves some way to do it. See, the government is always spending tax dollars coming up with new weapons. But what better killin' machine was ever created better than one of them dinosaurs? Heck, they was killin' machines! And I *know* they're here to get us. Quinlan there was just the first, unless we do something real sneaky. You up to sneaky, son?"

It was starting to make some kind of logical sense to Freeman now. He wasn't sure it was quite as simple as the colonel was suggesting to bring dinosaurs back to life. But *something* had killed Quin, and it was something he'd never seen before in his life. And now the colonel had a mission for him. "Sneaky, sir? You bet, sir!"

Colonel Denby grinned at him. "That's the spirit." He clapped him on the shoulder in a friendly manner. "And I think you'll like some of what I want you to do. I saw the way those girls in the camp were looking at you, and I know you looked back." Freeman was going to protest, but the colonel held up a hand. "And I don't blame you for it. I was a boy, too, once. Anyway, I think they're kind of stuck on you, and we can use that to our advantage. I want you to go over there, and talk with those girls. Act real friendly like. Be charming—I'm sure you can do that. And see if you can get them to tell you anything at all about what's going on out there. Take a peek anywhere they show you. Keep your eyes wide open, and report back to me."

"Yes, sir!" Freeman wasn't quite ready to believe yet that the two girls could be in on anything quite so nasty as the colonel seemed to imagine. They were probably just dupes, not aware of the true state of things. Maybe Freeman could show them the truth while he discovered it for himself.

"That's the spirit," Colonel Denby said approvingly. "And I know this duty ain't going to seem too hard for you to bear. But a man's got to do what a man's got to do, right?" He winked. "And you do what you have to. Just find out the truth, and bring it on back to me, hear?"

"Yes, sir!"

Sheriff Gates rubbed at the back of his neck. He was starting to tense up, and that was likely to give him one of his headaches. That he didn't need. He swallowed a couple of aspirins, and washed them down with a mouthful of tepid coffee. This was one hell of a place to live. You couldn't keep your coffee warm or your water cold. Still, it was his jurisdiction, and he was lucky to have this job. If there were any less people here, the area wouldn't need a permanent lawman anyway.

He didn't like being stuck in the middle of quarrels, but

he was firmly on the bull's-eye right now. On the one side, Denby and his crazy followers. On the other, that Professor Weiss and his university types. Both sides disliked one another, and each blamed the other for everything that happened. It was his job to figure out the truth in everything. Normally, that wasn't too hard to do, but in this case. . . . Both sides were being secretive, of that he was certain. The scientists maybe not deliberately, but they couldn't explain things in simple, clear language, which the sheriff preferred. Denby, now, the guy was paranoid, clean through to the bone. His followers, too.

They kept mostly to themselves, out in the desert a ways. Sheriff Gates knew they'd taken over an old farm that had played out thirty years earlier. There was barbed wire around it now, and rumors of armed patrols that he could readily believe in. Not technically legal, perhaps, but they minded their own business, mostly. The only way that the sheriff could check on them was to go in with a task force, and he had no intentions of trying that. Denby and his men were just waiting for that to happen, and they most likely had enough guns and supplies holed up in there to start a small war. Or maybe a major one. Sheriff Gates had seen what had happened in Waco on the TV, and he didn't want to turn Furnace into a second one of those.

So he had to defuse the current situation somehow. Weiss had said that he was going to be out here for two more months yet, and Gates knew that tempers were bound to blow before that was up. And in two months, Weiss and his team would be gone, maybe forever. But Denby and his men would remain. Gates wanted to be certain that they'd stay on good terms with the town. He didn't think Denby was crazy enough to try and invade the town. But with crazies . . . you never knew.

The best way to solve the problem, the sheriff decided,

was to figure out just who or what had killed the Brewsters' dog. He'd talked a lot with Bobby Marin, and was convinced that the kid hadn't done it. For one thing, he'd have needed a bowie knife or worse to cut up the dog the way it had been sliced open. And he hadn't been carrying one when the sheriff had found him. Nor had one turned up since. Anyway, only a powerful man could have overtaken a dog like that. Plus, some of the entrails had been missing, and the sheriff couldn't imagine even a perverted kid performing such a barbarous act. The Marin kid was probably just bored, but not warped.

Could Denby have done it? Without a doubt. The man was a fanatic, and if he'd had a reason then killing and butchering a dog wasn't beyond him. But did he *have* a reason? Besides, the kid hadn't seen a man do the killing; he'd seen an animal. But what kind of an animal could it have been? Bobby had probably just been affected by the film he'd been watching, and just *thought* it was a dinosaur. Maybe it had actually been a rabid coyote, or something? A mean coyote might attack and kill a dog.

His train of thought was cut off abruptly by the sound of a scream from down the street. It was a cry of pain and terror, but this time it wasn't a dog he was hearing. This was coming from some human throat.

Drawing his pistol, Sheriff Gates sprinted for the door to his small office. As he emerged into the desert night, he heard the scream again, fainter this time, but quite distinct. It had come from the Gimbal's house. The sheriff lumbered down the street. He was out of shape, and already his heart was pounding. He was out of breath. "Jesus," he panted, "I'll never make it." A couple of curious patrons poked their noses out of Chaney's as he ran by. No doubt they'd been drinking, Gates decided. Beers in hand, they trotted across the road after the Sheriff as he dashed around the back of the run-down Gimbal shack.

What the sheriff thought he saw was Old Man Gimbal pinned down on his back in his yard. And *something* was leaning over him. There wasn't much light out here, away from Main Street, and the sheriff could only make out an outline. "Damned coyote!" the sheriff grunted.

"Help!" the old man shrieked. The animal tore and slashed at his body, at his hands and his face. Sheriff Gates raised his gun and fired.

The creature screamed in rage and pain, jerking upward unexpectedly. It was about seven feet tall, and stood on two legs. A long tail swished behind it. It roared again, and whirled around, blood dripping from its mouth and from its shoulder. The sheriff had winged it. He fired a second time, still not believing what he was seeing. This was no coyote! It was bipedal, and *fast*. It dashed across the scraggly back-yard in the direction of the Thompson house. Gates didn't have a chance for another shot. He ran after it, but it was too late. The thing was gone.

Gates ran back to where Old Man Gimbal lay. He was dead alright. Practically torn to bits, like a rag doll. Just like the dog had been. Whatever this *thing* was, it was a killer, and now it had tasted human blood. The sheriff knew that it would be back for more if it wasn't stopped.

"Poor Gimbal," one of the patrons muttered.

Red Brody took a nervous gulp of his beer, not quite believing what he had seen. "You wounded the thing, Sheriff," he said. "But what the hell was it?"

"I don't know, Red," Gates admitted soberly. "But I do know it won't stop here." He stared down at Gimbal, and shook his head in sorrow. "He was a good man, and didn't deserve to die like this."

Red nodded. "Always told him to get rid of that outhouse and get indoor plumbing," he muttered. "I never thought it would be the death of him, though." He sighed, and took a swig of beer. "What now, Sheriff?"

Gates reholstered his gun. "We'd best get Gimbal inside. And tomorrow, I'm taking volunteers and we'll go hunting. We've got us a killer to nail."

CHAPTER 6

ALYSSA'S NIGHT HAD been disturbed by bad dreams. She hadn't been the only one; Caitlin had been tossing and turning, and crying out. She hadn't actually wakened, but whenever Alyssa had, Caitlin had been moaning or whimpering. Dr. West and Chelsea Ford, who shared the tent with them, had managed to sleep through everything. Well, they didn't seem to be as bothered by what was happening as Alyssa.

As the early morning sunlight started to warm the ground, Alyssa decided that she might as well get up and be first in the showers for a change. She couldn't get back to sleep, so she might as well get moving. Grabbing her towel and robe, she slid on her sandals and headed across to the facilities tent.

She was expecting the stand of trees to be larger, but the sheer size of it stunned her. The pines were about forty feet tall now—in one day! There were even small firs and willows growing. The area had spread again, but once more, away from the camp.

It was like living on the edge of a jungle. She could hear animal sounds from in the bushes, and shivered. Surely even Dr. Weiss would see that there was something terribly wrong now?

She used the tent, and then took a fast shower. Once she was back in the sleeping tent, she decided to chance irritating Dr. West and shook the older woman awake. "Come and see this," she said grimly.

Dr. West protested, but eventually followed Alyssa out. She stood, staring at the jungle. "Dear Lord," she murmured. "What's happening here?"

"I was kind of hoping that you might have a few ideas," Alyssa admitted. "I mean, I can tell that no way is that normal, but after that I'm totally stumped."

"To be honest," Dr. West said quietly, "so am I. I've never seen anything like that in my life."

"And there's animal life in there," Alyssa told her. "Caitlin and I found a pond last night with fish in it. Weird fish, more like insects than real fish. And if you listen carefully, you can hear animals calling to one another. And none of that was there yesterday morning."

Dr. West shook her head as if trying to clear it. "The growth must have attracted animals from the neighborhood," she suggested. "There's got to be food and water in there for them."

"How could it attract *fish*?" Alyssa demanded. "They couldn't exactly swim here, you know!"

"I know," Dr. West agreed, her shoulders drooping. "Maybe we should organize a hunt, and see what we can find in there."

"It's not very safe," Alyssa pointed out. "Caitlin was

bitten by a fish. And who knows what else might be in there? Snakes, scorpions, coyotes . . .''

"Answers?" suggested Dr. West. She shielded her eyes. "Look, there are birds, too." There were winged shapes fluttering across the sky over the trees. "They look a bit odd, though."

"Everything around here's looking a bit odd," Alyssa pointed out. "Maybe we should call in some specialists?"

Dr. West smiled ruefully. "I *am* a specialist."

Alyssa flushed with embarrassment.

"Don't worry," Dr. West said. "I was only joking. And you're right. Come on." Still in her bathrobe, she led the way to her work tent, and started to power up the computer. "I can send an E-mail to the department, and see if one of the zoologists would like to come out and take a look at this." She clicked the mouse on the internet-symbol, and immediately got an error message. "Damn. The phone line's still out. This stupid town . . .''

"We could try going into Furnace and calling," Alyssa suggested. "There's a public phone in Chaney's store."

"Good idea," Dr. West agreed. She drove Alyssa to Furnace in her Jeep, rattling most of the way. It was still early, but most of the town was awake. Alyssa followed Dr. West into the store, where she made straight for the public phone. After jiggling it a couple of times, she scowled.

"No dial tone. Great." Dr. West replaced the receiver, and walked to the counter. "The phone's dead," she pointed out. "Is there another I could use?"

Chaney shrugged. "No public one. You might ask the sheriff if you can use his. It's county paid-for, after all."

"Thanks," Dr. West said dryly. She and Alyssa headed out of the store. Alyssa grabbed the woman's arm.

"Just a second," she said. She darted around the back of the store to where the greenhouse was, and stared.

THE INVADERS • 53

The greenhouse had been shattered, and there were plants all over the back area now. At least half an acre, spreading out into the desert. Ferns, pines, even oaks. And more of the large insects. There was a noise behind her, and then Dr. West said: "We're not the only one with a private jungle, it appears."

"I'll bet it's like this all over town," Alyssa suggested, as they headed for the sheriff's office. "Whatever's making this stuff grow, it's going wild fast."

"No bet," Dr. West deadpanned. She knocked on the door of the sheriff's office, and then went inside.

Sheriff Gates was loading a double-barreled shotgun with huge shells. Alyssa shivered as she saw it. He glanced up. "Morning, ladies. This isn't a good time to be visiting, even if you have got complaints."

"Nothing like that, Sheriff," Dr. West answered. "It's just that the public phone's dead in the store, and I wanted to try and get in touch with the university."

He gestured at the phone on his desk. "Be my guest."

She walked over and picked it up, cradling the receiver. Then, with a sigh, replaced it. "That's dead, too."

"Two phones dead in one morning?" Sheriff Gates didn't look happy.

"Three," Alyssa corrected him. "The computer line at our camp's down, too." She raised an eyebrow. "I don't suppose anybody thinks this is coincidental, do they?"

"No they don't," the sheriff answered, glowering. "Somebody's cut the lines, that much is obvious. And if it had been your group doing it, you wouldn't have come here making it obvious. Which kind of leaves me only one suspect."

"Denby," Dr. West said.

"Right." Sheriff Gates sighed. "I think the colonel's just had himself an acute fit of paranoia. I suppose I'm going to have to go and have words with him, just as soon as the hunt is over. Sorry for the inconvenience, ma'am.''

"*Inconvenience?*" repeated Dr. West. "We're cut off from the outside world. That's more than an *inconvenience.*"

"Then I suggest you drive on over to Farlow Creek," the sheriff said. "It's only about an hour's drive. "You could call from there.''

"I suppose so," agreed Dr. West. She glanced at Alyssa. "We'd better go back to camp first, though, and tell Dr. Weiss. He'll be annoyed at the delay, but I'm starting to think we're going to need some help here soon."

Alyssa nodded, and then started to follow her out. At the door, she hesitated, and asked the sheriff: "Just what are you hunting, by the way?"

"Can't rightly say," he admitted. "Some kind of animal. It killed Old Man Gimbal last night and started snacking on the body. I managed to wing it, so with a bit of luck we can track it now it's daylight. You and the doctor take care, hear? It's tasted human blood, and it's wounded. It may be very dangerous."

Wonderful, thought Alyssa. *Now we've got a wounded cougar or something to watch out for, too. Just what we needed.*

Dr. West was silent all the way back to the dig. Alyssa was trying to make some sort of sense out of everything that was happening, and was not getting very far with it. Those idiotic militia people hadn't helped matters at all by cutting the phone lines. But they couldn't possibly be behind the odd jungles. That was *way* out of their league. Alyssa giggled.

"What's so funny?" asked Dr. Gates.

Alyssa smiled. "I was just thinking how ridiculous it is that Denby is always suspecting the government is behind everything odd that happens. Maybe he's right, after all.''

They looked at one another, and burst out laughing.

Back at the camp, Dr. West went off after Caitlin's father. Alyssa found her friend. "Feel like a trip?" she asked. "We're headed over to Farlow Creek." She explained about the phones.

"Sounds like a break from this place, at least," Caitlin agreed. She scratched at her palm. "Count me in."

Dr. Weiss didn't like losing workers for the morning, but he had apparently agreed with bad grace to the trip. Even he couldn't deny that there was something odd about the jungle on the outskirts of the dig. "Straight out and back," he told Dr. West, Alyssa and Caitlin. "This isn't a shopping trip, or a boy hunt, understand?"

"I think we can be trusted," Dr. West said dryly. She was obviously very irritated with his attitude. "Come along, girls."

Caitlin rolled her eyes. "Dad's in a bad mood today," she muttered.

"Another egg's been broken," Dr. West explained. "Even locked away, somebody managed to smash it. I've had to put the final two in a safe."

"You think that will help?" Alyssa asked.

"Nobody can get into it to break them," Dr. West said firmly. She started the Jeep, and headed down toward the jungle patch. "Well, the road's this way," she said cheerfully. "We may as well see how far this stuff extends while we're at it, eh?"

Alyssa didn't like being close to the forest at all, but she was sure there was nothing to really worry about. After all, they were in a Jeep, and there wasn't much that could catch them in that. Not even a man-eating cougar, or whatever it was. Still, she watched the trees warily, still scared. There was something terribly wrong about the place. Normally, she adored forests. There was so much to see and paint, the artist in her loved the trees. But not this forest, and not these trees. They gave her the shakes.

There was something flying over the trees, high on the wing. She couldn't quite make it out, but it looked wrong. Nudging Caitlin, who was scratching her palm again, she gestured upward. It was difficult to see against the sun, but the silhouette looked very odd. "What kind of a bird is that?"

Caitlin shaded her eyes, and scowled. "It's pretty large. Must be a raptor of some sort. Hawk, maybe, or even an eagle. But . . ." She shook her head. "The wings look wrong, and the head's all odd. I wish it was closer."

"I don't," Alyssa said firmly. "I wish it weren't here at all."

"Let me have a look," Dr. West said. She pulled the Jeep to a halt, and then stared up at the sky. She frowned, and then looked worried. "It's . . . No, it can't be." She glanced at Alyssa, troubled. "It's got the configuration of a pterosaur, which is impossible."

Alyssa knew what that meant: a flying dinosaur. Some of them managed to get pretty big, she remembered. Forty feet or so across . . . That thing was high; it was possible that it might be that size.

Except it should have been extinct for the past sixty million years or so. . . .

"It can't be a dinosaur," Caitlin argued.

"You're telling me that?" asked Dr. West. Her voice sounded very shaky. "Please! I *know* it can't be. But it *looks* like one . . ."

There was a snort from the edge of the jungle, and Alyssa whirled to see what had caused it. She stiffened in shock, and her hand shook as she pointed. "I think *that* looks like one, too."

It was standing, glaring at them, almost six feet tall. A long tail was held out horizontally behind it. Its long arms ended in nasty-looking claws. It stood on two toes of its feet; a third extended forward, equipped with a five-inch long, sickle-shaped talon. The mouth was slightly open as it breathed, showing large, pointed teeth. A wattle hung from its neck. It was a greenish brown color, lighter on the belly.

"Dear God," whispered Dr. West. "It looks like *Deinonychus*."

"It looks like trouble to me," Alyssa breathed. "Maybe we should get going. *Now!*"

Dr. West hastily slammed the Jeep into drive, and released the brake.

As she did, the *Deinonychus* moved, faster than Alyssa had ever imagined possible. It ran and then leaped for the sluggishly moving vehicle, both feet off the ground. The claws slammed into the side of the Jeep, and the dinosaur roared. She wasn't sure whether from pain or anger. Metal screamed and tore, and the creature ripped its feet free, scrambling to grab its fleeing prey.

There was the stench of gasoline, and Alyssa realized the animal's attack had ruptured the gas tank. Then the *Deinonychus* threw itself at them again.

Alyssa tumbled down, dragging Caitlin with her. The terrible claws slashed through the seat leather, and the dinosaur wobbled as it stood on the side of the vehicle. Alyssa lashed out with her foot, kicking it hard in the stomach. With a howl, it toppled from the car.

And the engine spluttered, and then died.

The Jeep ran on for a short distance, as Alyssa almost stopped breathing. The gasoline had poured out of the slashed side, and they were stranded there. She glanced back out of the Jeep, and saw the *Deinonychus* stagger to its feet again, hissing angrily. It staggered slightly, but then regained its balance and moved forward.

It could see that its prey was incapable of escape, and it was hunting them. . . .

CHAPTER 7

ALYSSA WAS ON the verge of panic, but she tried to keep her head. She'd been talking about the possibility of dinosaurs coming back to life somehow, but *seeing* one was still a shock. Especially since it was clear that the creature in question saw them as food. Naturally, there were no guns or anything like that in the Jeep, but there was a heavy shovel. She snatched it up, and stood facing the advancing *Deinonychus*.

"You can't fight it off with that!" Dr. West exclaimed, futilely trying to restart the vehicle.

"Well, we don't have any dynamite," complained Alyssa, not taking her eyes off the dinosaur for a second. "It's this or sprinkle salt on ourselves and lay down and wait to be eaten!" She whirled the shovel about, to show the creature she meant business.

It didn't seem to be impressed. Hissing and growling low in its throat, it padded forward, clicking its claws. This was obviously meant to intimidate its prey, and Alyssa could testify that it worked.

Then it leaped, its feet forward, those two lethal-looking talons aimed directly at Alyssa's body. With a howl of her own, Alyssa swung the shovel and brought the heavy blade across the dinosaur's left shoulder, slamming hard against its arm. Pain juddered through her arms as she made contact, but not as much as must have gone through the dinosaur. It screeched, and fell from the back of the Jeep to the desert floor, stunned. Her fingers tingling, and adrenaline coursing through her body, Alyssa leaped into the back of the Jeep, looking down at the *Deinonychus*, and whirled the shovel around for another blow.

But this thing was smart; it was dazed, but it didn't simply lay there feeling sorry for itself. As she brought the blade down toward its head, it lunged forward, its teeth-filled mouth barely missing her fingers. It closed over the handle, shredding it to matchsticks. The shovel disintegrated in her hands, the metal blade dropping to the dry earth.

Alyssa threw the mangled shovel handle at the creature and frantically searched the Jeep for something—*anything*—to use as a weapon. There wasn't anything at all suitable, and the lizard was getting its breath back for another attack. Alyssa noticed that it carried its left arm limply at its side. I must have broken it, Alyssa thought. The only problem was that Alyssa knew the *Deinonychus* killed with its hind feet. It would have no trouble killing her, but it would have a problem eating her afterward. Terrific.

"We've got to try and run for the trees!" Caitlin cried. "Maybe we can climb one before it gets to us!"

"I wouldn't want to bet on it," Alyssa answered. But she didn't have any better ideas.

"Two of us might make it," Dr. West said grimly. She'd abandoned all hope of starting the Jeep again. "You two move, fast. I'll stay here and keep it distracted." She gave an odd smile. "It's at times like this I wish I hadn't given up smoking." When Alyssa looked at her blankly, she pointed to the spilled gasoline. "Then we could set that alight."

Suddenly, Alyssa had an idea. A crazy, ridiculous idea. Before she lost her nerve she jumped from the Jeep and snatched up the shovel's blade.

"Alyssa!" shouted Caitlin.

"Come back here!" screamed Dr. West. "What are you doing?"

"Sparks!" answered Alyssa. She clanged the blade against the side of the Jeep. Nothing happened.

She struck with the blade again, and again.

The *Deinonychus* snarled, and staggered to its feet. Frantically, Alyssa swung the shovel blade again. This time the edge screeched along the vehicle, and a shower of sparks fountained out.

With a *whoomp,* the gasoline caught fire. Flames shot up almost eight feet in the air, thankfully between her and the monster. It howled and leaped back, its toes singed by the flames. Dr. West pushed Caitlin hard.

"Move!" she screamed. "The Jeep will go up next!" They both sprinted for the closest trees. Alyssa had to circle the Jeep to join them. There wasn't more than a thin coating of gasoline left in the tank, but it was enough to catch fire, and start the vehicle blazing, too. At least there was no chance of it exploding.

Alyssa ran, and glanced back over her shoulder.

The *Deinonychus* was streaking after them. It had angled to go after the one in the lead—Caitlin. It must be hoping that this would make the other two humans veer away, so it could take them down separately before they could reach cover.

"Caitlin!" Alyssa screamed. "It's after you!"

Caitlin had just reached the edge of the jungle. She looked back and yelped in fear as she saw the killer lizard closing on her far faster than she could run. She stumbled, and fell, whimpering, and then rolled over to try and get back to her feet.

And the *Deinonychus* was on her. Alyssa wanted to scream, but she didn't have the breath for it. They had no weapons, and there was no escape for her friend. She was going to see Caitlin ripped to pieces right in front of her.

Then, astoundingly, the creature paused and snuffled. It was inches away from Caitlin, its huge, scythelike claws ready to disembowel her. And it stopped, dead, in its tracks. Its nostrils flared, and it seemed to be smelling her.

And, even more amazingly, it turned away from Caitlin, ignoring her completely to spring for Dr. West instead.

There was no time to analyze this weird behavior. It had spared Caitlin's life, but it obviously had no intention of sparing anyone else. Dr. West threw up her hands in a futile attempt to protect herself. There was nothing Alyssa could do but keep running and pray she could make it to a tree herself before the thing came after her.

Then there was the sound of a gunshot, and the *Deinonychus* screamed. Blood splattered from its right shoulder, and the force of the bullet whipped the monster back. A second shot blasted its right eye to pieces, showering Dr. West with ichor and blood.

The dinosaur heaved a sigh, and collapsed to the ground in a bleeding heap.

Alyssa staggered to a halt, wheezing for breath.

Beyond the flames of the burning Jeep, Freeman stood alertly, legs spread, pistol in both hands, alert for any further movement. Beyond him was the humvee. She'd been concentrating so hard on running, she hadn't even heard it approach.

"I never thought I'd be so happy to see a gun nut in my life," she muttered. Slowly, she walked forward to where Dr. West was hyperventilating. Alyssa couldn't blame her; the woman had been within seconds of being brutally murdered. Grabbing her arms, Alyssa shook the scientist hard. Gradually, Dr. West calmed down again, and started to breath normally. But she was shaking violently.

"I'm . . . all right," she gasped finally. "I'm sorry."

"Nothing to be sorry about, ma'am," Freeman said, joining them. He stared down at the dinosaur he'd killed. "You're just lucky I was out after you, that's all."

"After us?" Alyssa asked. "Why?"

He blushed. "Well, you *did* say you'd like to see me again."

"You don't know how glad I was to see you!" Alyssa assured him. Leaning forward, she kissed his cheek. "Thank you; you literally saved our lives."

Freeman blushed again. "Is your friend okay?"

"Let's check." They hurried over to Caitlin, who was still dazedly staring at the dead *Deinonychus*. "Snap out of it," Alyssa said. "You've been taken off the menu."

Caitlin shuddered. "I stared into its face," she said faintly. "I could feel its breath on my cheek. Smell the blood on its breath. *It didn't kill me.*"

"No," agreed Dr. West, having recovered her poise. "It didn't. And I don't know why. Not that I'm not very happy, of course. But there was no reason for it to spare you."

"Maybe it's got a thing for redheads?" Alyssa joked. "Anyway, can we pick this discussion up later? I *really* think it would be a good idea to get out of here before its relatives decide to stop by for a family reunion and barbecue.''

"Come on," Freeman said. He had his pistol at the alert. "I'll watch, you three retreat."

Alyssa helped Caitlin to her feet. "Come on," she urged her friend. "Let's get moving. The next dinosaur along might not be as picky about who he eats."

She didn't feel safe until they were inside the humvee and the doors were locked. Dr. West got in the front beside Freeman, and Alyssa stayed with Caitlin in the back, hugging her shaking friend tightly. Freeman put his pistol away finally, and started the motor. "You were going to Farlow Creek, right?" he asked.

"Not anymore," Dr. West said firmly. "We have to get back and warn the others about the *Deinonychus*. If there's one, there may be more."

Freeman gave Dr. West an odd look. "They don't know about the dinosaurs?" he asked.

"Of course not," Dr. West said, obviously confused. "Nobody knew about the beasts. Why should they?"

"Alyssa guessed," Caitlin said. "She thinks they're hatching from those eggs."

"The *eggs*?" Dr. West laughed. It sounded rather forced, though. "That *Deinonychus* couldn't have been inside one of those eggs. It would have to be several years old to be that size."

"I don't think it could have been running around in the desert for years without being noticed," Alyssa objected. "And the first we heard about it was that it may have been the creature that killed the dog in town the other night."

"Then what are you saying?" asked Dr. West.

"I don't know what I'm saying," Alyssa replied. "Just that those hollow eggs broke before this all began—the forest, the dinosaurs and all."

"It has to be a coincidence," Dr. West insisted.

"The colonel doesn't believe in coincidences," Freeman said gently. "He says that they're just connections you haven't figured out yet."

"And just what has *he* figured out?" asked Dr. West rather huffily.

Freeman looked embarrassed again. "Well, ma'am . . . He did kind of think that you knew about the dinosaurs, and that you were making them."

"That's absolute nonsense!" Dr. West snapped.

"Well, I'm kind of inclined to agree with you this time," Freeman admitted. "After all, if you know about them, you'd hardly have gone that close to one, would you? At least, not without a weapon."

Alyssa was starting to put two and two together. One paranoid militia colonel, and one convenient rescue. And Freeman had mentioned he was looking for them. "He sent you out to spy on us, didn't he?" she asked.

Once again, Freeman blushed, the back of his neck going red, confirming her guess. "It was just an excuse for me to see you again," Freeman insisted. Alyssa was touched, because she could see that this was at least half the truth.

"I'm glad you came," she told him. "For whatever reason."

"Me too," he admitted.

Not sure what else to say, Alyssa glanced down at Caitlin, who was uncharacteristically quiet. Even granting the fact that she'd almost been killed, Alyssa would expect her friend to be chattering away. Instead, she was scratching away at her palm again, her eyes slightly unfocused.

"You okay?" Alyssa asked her, grabbing her friend's wrist to stop her scratching. "You're going to draw blood if you keep that up."

"It *itches*," Caitlin snapped, pulling herself free, and scratching again.

"What does?" Dr. West asked. "Did you fall and sting yourself, or something?"

"Last night," Alyssa explained. "She was bitten by a fish. I dressed the wound, but it seems to be irritating her."

"A *fish*?"

"I told you. There's a pond in there," Alyssa explained. "Maybe more than one. It had fish in it, and one of them nipped Caitlin."

"Maybe there's an infection," Dr. West said, worried. "I'll give her some antibiotics when we get back to camp."

Alyssa nodded. She hadn't really thought the bite had been that bad. But now she wondered. If there were dinosaurs alive, maybe there were prehistoric microbes, too? She'd heard about Native Americans being killed off by diseases like measles they'd never met before and against which they had no immunity. Was it possible that Caitlin had been infected with some strange bug? She was really getting worried when they reached camp.

Dr. West took Caitlin off for an injection, while Alyssa went after Dr. Weiss. Freeman came with her, and she was glad. It would help having somebody to back up her story.

"Back already?" Dr. Weiss asked, looking up from the dig area he was working.

"Forget about digging up dinosaur bones," Alyssa told him. "There are plenty of living ones out there." She gestured at the forest growth. "We were attacked by a *Deinonychus*."

"What?" He straightened up and stared at her in astonishment. "This is no time for joking."

"I'm not joking. It totaled the Jeep, and nearly totalled *us*. Thankfully, Freeman stopped it with some really nice target shooting."

"It's true, sir," Freeman confirmed. "It's laid out dead in the desert if you want to have a look at it."

Dr. Weiss shook his head, obviously reluctant to believe it. "Dr. West?" he asked. "Caitlin?"

Interesting who he asked for first, Alyssa realized. Not his daughter. "Dr. Weiss is giving Caitlin a shot. She was bitten by a fish yesterday, and it's bothering her."

"A fish?" Dr. Weiss looked like he'd had one too many blows to the head in a boxing match. He couldn't keep up with this. "What's going on?"

"Survival," Freeman said bluntly. "How many weapons do you have?"

"Weapons?" Caitlin's father shook his head. "Why would we need weapons?"

"Because you can't stop dinosaurs with shovels," Alyssa snapped. "I know; I tried it." She turned to Freeman. "I'm sure you guys must have stockpiles of weapons enough to take out an army," she said. "Do you think Colonel Denby would help?"

"I'm sure he would," Freeman answered. "I can go ask him."

"Great." Alyssa turned to Dr. Weiss. "And we have to warn the folks in town. Sheriff Gates is off hunting a dinosaur, but I don't think he knows it. He thinks it's a rabid coyote, or a cougar or something. We have to let everyone know what they're up against."

"Then we have to get word out," Freeman said, echoing her own thoughts. "Maybe call in the Army or something to take them out."

"*Them*?" asked Dr. Weiss, getting his wits back at last. "What are you talking about? How many *is* "them"?"

"I don't know," admitted Alyssa. "We only saw the one *Deinonychus*."

"You saw *what*?" thundered Dr. Weiss.

"A deinonychus," answered Alyssa calmly. "But since it was looking for take-out and we were catch of the day, we didn't stop around to see how many friends it had brought with it."

"You saw *one* wild animal that you misidentified as an extinct dinosaur and you're panicking?" Dr. Weiss demanded. "Aren't you overreacting?"

Alyssa stared at him in amazement. "Hey, after you've been chased as prey, *then* you can tell me I'm overreacting! I could have been killed. Ask them if I'm overreacting."

"You can't plan on *killing* these creatures," Dr. Weiss said. "If there really *are* dinosaurs out there, we should study them. Think of what we could learn."

"*You* think," Alyssa replied. "I'm all for forming circles out of the wagons and loading up on all the guns we can find." She turned back to Freeman. "How about dynamite?" she asked. "Cannons? Nuclear missiles?"

Freeman laughed. "The Colonel would just have *loved* one of those," he said. "We've got plenty of firepower, though. Don't worry—we can take care of anything once we're mobilized."

"I believe it," Alyssa answered. "Thanks, Freeman. I owe you. We all owe you." She kissed his cheek again, and watched him blush. She'd discovered a new sport to enjoy. He really was incredibly naive where girls were concerned. Ah, well, at least she could get *some* fun out of this situation.

Freeman waved, and hurried back to the humvee. Alyssa forgot about him for the moment, and turned back to Dr. Weiss. He still had a dreamy expression on his face, and she realized that he was thinking about the possibility of meeting a dinosaur in the flesh.

What he didn't seem to be able to get through his thick

skull was that *flesh* was what they were after. His, hers and anyone's.

"We've got to get working," she told him urgently. "These things seem to be getting bolder. They attacked the dog under cover of darkness last night, but they attacked our Jeep in broad daylight." She pointed to the edge of the jungle. "They're probably out there now, watching us and getting ready to order dinner. We've got to get ready for an attack."

"Attack?" Dr. Weiss stared at her in amazement. "My dear Miss Baker, there's no need to panic."

"There's *every* need to panic!" she yelled. "These things eat meat. And *we're* meat! We're also spread out and incapable of defending ourselves before Freeman gets back with weapons. So unless you want your students turned into sushi, let's start getting everyone together and see if we can improvise some means of defending ourselves."

"Look, young lady," Dr. Weiss said, giving her a pained look. "I'm sure you're just allowing your fears to run away with you—"

"She's *not,*" said Dr. West with emphasis. "Sam, forgive me, but you're an idiot. We were almost killed today. Alyssa is quite correct. We've got to start getting defensive. Oh, and your daughter is fine, in case you're interested. I gave her sleeping tablets, so she could get some rest." Dr. Weiss looked as though he were about to explode with indignation. Dr. West sighed. "Can the complaints, Sam," she said. "Or do we do this without your help?"

"You make it sound like we were about to be besieged, or something," he complained.

"That's exactly what I think is going to happen," Dr. West replied grimly. "So we'd better be ready, hadn't we?"

CHAPTER 8

SHERIFF GATES WAS badly worried. He had been searching around Furnace for any further tracks from the animal that had killed Old Man Gimbal, without any luck. The only tracks had been in that small area that had been watered. And they hadn't looked like anything he'd ever hunted before in his life.

What he *had* seen in town disturbed him greatly. The odd patches of fern that the girl from the dinosaur dig had noticed had grown bigger. A *lot* bigger. The one out back of Chaney's was now almost two acres out into the desert. Even the ones that had started in pots had spread across the ground somehow. And it wasn't just ferns anymore—there were trees, grasses and plants and even flowers. Aside from a few straggly geraniums or a tomato plant here and there, he hadn't ever seen any vegetation in Furnace. Except if you considered dried flowers vegetation.

And yet somehow Furnace had overnight turned into a lush tropical forest. It just wasn't right. It disturbed his sense of order. And that spelled trouble.

Still toting his shotgun, he walked slowly around the whole town. Funny, he thought. These patches of greenery should have brightened the place up. And him, too. Instead, it made him nervous. Maybe he'd just spent too much time staring at rocks.

There was a rattling noise, and he jerked up the shotgun. Then he forced himself to calm down. The sound had come from trash cans beside the Hanrahan house. It was just some cat digging in there for scraps, nothing more. He had to stop imagining things. Going over to the can, he slammed the butt of the shotgun on its side. "Get out of there!" he yelled.

It did. But it wasn't a cat. It was some kind of a lizard. Worse, it was running on its back feet, its fore feet in the air, clutching some scraps of fatty meat. It hissed at him as it scuttled away.

What the heck? He'd *never* seen a lizard on its back feet before. Come to think of it, he'd never even heard of any that could do that kind of thing.

And that made him realize something else odd about the town: he hadn't seen a single cat all day. Normally, there were five or six scrounging for food, laying on porches or just ambling about like they owned the place. Not today. He hadn't seen one.

No dogs, either.

The Brewsters' dog had been killed, but what about the others? Not only hadn't he seen any, he'd not heard a bark or anything.

Sheriff Gates was beginning to get really spooked. There were too many things out of the ordinary happening, and that bothered him. The problem was, he couldn't get a handle on the whole thing. None of it made any sense to him.

What was going on in Furnace? And why?

Freeman winced under the scrutiny of Colonel Denby. He'd reported in and passed along Alyssa's request for aid, certain that the colonel would agree. Only . . . he hadn't. He simply walked up and down his office, thinking. That bothered Freeman, but not as much as the look the colonel suddenly gave him.

"You going soft, boy?" the colonel demanded in a quiet voice.

"Soft, sir? Me?" Freeman shook his head. "No, sir!"

"Then how come you fell for the story those *females* fed you?" the colonel asked. "A couple of pretty faces turned your brains to mush, soldier?"

Freeman blushed, thinking of the two pretty faces. "No, sir," he denied. "I know I kept my head."

"Like Hades," the colonel growled. "Freeman, I *told* you those government agents are sneaky. Don't you listen to me anymore?"

"Of course I do, sir!" Freeman protested.

"But you got suckered anyway." He sighed. "These government agents want us to come out to their camp with our weapons? Boy, can't you *see* yourself being suckered? Did you expect them to paint the word *trap* on it first?"

"Sir," Freeman objected, "this isn't a trap. They really do need our help."

The colonel shook his head sadly. "I *told* you they made these dinosaurs. It's a ploy to get us all out there where we can be either attacked or arrested. And you're so dumb you virtually held the gun to your own head."

Freeman was shocked by this. "But, sir . . . I *saw* the girls in trouble. They were about to be killed! That was no trick!"

"They no doubt had backup ready to save them," the colonel answered. "They set fire to their Jeep to draw you in, and staged the whole thing. They took you in real good, didn't they? A pretty face, and all your training goes for nothing. It's a trap, boy, as plain as that ugly nose on your face, and you're too jackassed intent on the girls that you don't see the obvious."

Freeman shook his head. "Sir, you didn't see their faces. They were terrified."

"And you said that the dinosaur caught one of them and let her go again!" The colonel threw his hands up. "If that doesn't tell you they were faking, what more do you need? A sign from God himself? Use whatever brains they haven't addled on you, boy. We're not budging from this farm, and they aren't going to sucker us out or force us out." He spun about. "That's all, soldier."

"But, sir," Freeman started to protest.

"I *said* that's all," snapped Colonel Denby.

Freeman saluted. "Yes, sir." Wheeling about, he marched from the room. Outside the office, his shoulders slumped.

Was it possible that the colonel was right? Had Alyssa and Caitlin been the bait to lure him in? Were they planning to get the militia to their camp either to arrest them or to set the dinosaurs on them?

No. He couldn't believe it. The girls and the woman with them had been terrified. They couldn't have faked that. And he had seen no sign of backup protecting them; the opposite, in fact. The rest of their people had been back at their camp. But if the girls *hadn't* been lying to him, then that meant only one thing.

The colonel was wrong.

Freeman didn't know what to do. He'd always believed that the colonel was right about everything. He always made everything so clear and so simple. There were no problems when he'd explained things. But . . . if he *could* be wrong about this . . .

What else might he be wrong about?

Gnawed at by uncertainty, Freeman discovered that he was walking toward the armory without really thinking about it. If Colonel Denby was wrong, and this wasn't a trap, then the university party was going to be in desperate need of help, and of weapons. And only he could help them. He couldn't help recalling the kiss that Alyssa had given him. Not come-ons, like the colonel claimed. Just a kiss between friends. Alyssa and Caitlin wouldn't lie to him, not deliberately. He was certain of that.

Maybe the colonel *was* right, and he *was* being a fool. But he simply couldn't stand around and do nothing. He was certain that would be the same as allowing the girls to die. If the colonel wasn't going to act, then it was up to him.

Freeman realized what that meant: he was disobeying orders. The colonel would have every right to have him shot for it. He was risking his life in faith that Alyssa wasn't lying to him. And even if she wasn't, the colonel wasn't one to forgive an offense. If Freeman left the building now, he was disobeying the colonel's orders. Whether he was right or wrong to do so was irrelevant; you simply *didn't* disobey.

Which, he realized, in one way was a good thing. It meant that nobody would question whatever he did. They'd just assume that he was following orders.

Realizing that he had, somehow, made up his mind, Freeman walked along with resolve in his step. If he was going to do this, he'd better do it right. He reached the barn that had been converted into the armory and rapped on the door. Semanski was on duty, and Freeman saluted. ''I have to get supplies for a raid,'' he informed Semanski.

The other man grinned. "Action at last?" he asked in anticipation. "This should be fun. So, what do you need?"

Freeman considered. The scientists weren't likely to be too familiar with weapons, so he needed stuff even an idiot couldn't go wrong using. "A case of grenades," he decided. He added four pistols, six rifles, ammunition, and a couple of flare guns. In the event of trouble they couldn't handle, maybe they could signal for help. Semanski helped him to carry this all to the humvee.

"Boy, have I been waiting for this," he said happily.

"You'll have to wait some more," Freeman told him. "You're still on duty for two more hours."

Semanski's face fell. "Yeah, you're right. Rats. I get to miss all of the fun. Well, enjoy it, Freeman."

"I'll try." Freeman didn't think that what was coming was likely to be fun. "You keep your eyes peeled for anything . . . unusual," he added. He couldn't warn the man about dinosaurs without sounding crazy. But he couldn't just walk away without saying something. "There have been some odd things seen around in the past few days."

"Damned FBI, no doubt," Semanski growled. He patted his gun. "I'll be ready for anything."

"You'd better be," Freeman said softly. He started up the humvee, and drove over to where Horse was always kept in a run, looking for his dog. Well, technically, Horse was the colonel's, but Freeman had always taken care of him. He really loved the dog, and he was kind of pleased that Horse had taken to Alyssa, too.

There was no sign of the dog. There was, however, a tear in the chicken-wire enclosure big enough for Horse to have slipped out. Freeman frowned. The dog knew his duty as well as any of the men; he'd never run away. Besides, he could never have made a gash like that. For a second,

Freeman wondered if some government agent had snuck in and gone for Horse. But that didn't make sense. Nobody could have entered the perimeter of the farm undetected. And Horse would never have allowed anyone close to him without barking an alarm. And he surely hadn't done that.

Puzzled and disturbed, Freeman drove to the guard post at the gate. He gave the correct password, and was allowed to drive out. Realizing he was cutting ties with the only people in the world that he respected and cared for, he drove away without looking back. It was the hardest thing he had ever done in his life.

If he *had* looked back, he'd have seen the colonel and Semanski watching him leave. Semanski was troubled.

"You were right, Colonel," he said, as if he didn't want to believe it. "He *has* deserted. Freeman, of all people." He shook his head.

"They're damned sneaky," the colonel said grimly. "They got to him through his weakness. That boy just wants a girl way too badly."

Semanski nodded. "But . . . why did you let him go, Colonel?" he asked, confused. "We could have stopped him."

"Because we're going after him," the colonel explained. "When he gets to their camp, he's going to let them know that their little ruse failed. They're going to have to rethink, and regroup. *That's* when we strike, when they're not ready. Assemble the men, Semanski, we're going to hunt us some Feds."

Caitlin awoke feeling feverish. She was in a tent, on a camp bed, but she couldn't make much more sense of things like that. Her memory seemed to be fuzzy, and her body very sick. She felt wave after wave of nausea sweep through her, wanting to be sick, but knowing she wouldn't be. Her head felt like it was splitting open, and she found it hard to concentrate on anything.

There was a burning itching sensation in her palm, and she focused sufficiently to scratch at it, digging her nails deep into the skin, looking for peace. To her astonishment, no blood welled up as she tore at herself with her nails. Instead, the skin peeled away, flaking off to the floor.

Underneath it . . .

Caitlin stared in horror.

There was new skin there, but nothing like the old. It was rough, and greenish in color . . . She shook with fear.

What was happening to her?

Dr. West ran a hand through her hair, and ducked to enter the sleeping tent. She had to check up on Caitlin, to see how she was doing. She liked the young girl, and worried about her; it was a shame her own father didn't. Dr. Weiss could be so self-absorbed; she could see why his wife must have left him. He was only interested in his work, and everything else came later. Much later. He hadn't even stopped in to see how his daughter was doing. Right now, he was organizing a closedown of fieldwork under strong protest. He didn't dare actually call Dr. West and Alyssa liars after they'd told their stories, but he looked as if he wanted to do so.

What an arrogant, unsympathetic idiot! Well, if *he* didn't care about Caitlin, other people did. She'd check on her first, and then go and examine the last remaining egg, and see if . . .

The bed where she'd left Caitlin sleeping was empty.

Dr. West blinked, and stared at it, confused. She'd given Caitlin a sleeping tablet that should have kept her out for hours yet. She couldn't have moved out by herself. Besides, where would she go? Dr. West crossed to the bed. The covers had been thrown back, and there were papery thin flakes all over the sheets. Dr. West couldn't make out what it could possibly be. But it reminded her of discarded snake skin.

Had someone come into the camp and taken Caitlin? But who would do such a thing? And why? Dr. West looked around the tent, puzzled, looking for any sign of what might have happened. Nothing was disturbed except the bed. However, Caitlin had left the tent, and it had to have been by the main entrance. She walked over to it, looking for anything at all. There were no footprints, of course, in the baked ground.

By the entrance was some more of the white flakes. And, more ominous, scattered clumps of red hair. She bent to examine it, confused. It was as if someone had grabbed a handful of Caitlin's hair and yanked it out of her scalp. But *why*? And how could it have been done without poor Caitlin screaming in pain?

The thought that a dinosaur might have snuck into camp and attacked Caitlin chilled her for a second. Then she realized that this couldn't have happened. There was no sign of blood at all. If Caitlin had been attacked, there would have been lots of it.

No. Whatever had happened to Caitlin, she'd either walked or been taken out of the tent.

But why? And where to? And by whom?

CHAPTER 9

ALYSSA WAS JUST about exhausted. It had taken every last ounce of her persuasive abilities to convince Dr. Weiss that there was something seriously wrong. He'd been reluctant to accept the idea that there were living dinosaurs until Donovan had given a cry and pointed upward.

Flying over the camp was something that looked superficially like a bird. But it was far larger than any bird, had a long, thin tail, and a bony ridge extending back from its head.

"*Pterandon,*" Dr. Weiss breathed, his face illuminated by his discovery. But at least it had proven that Alyssa wasn't mistaken or lying. Using this as leverage, she and Dr. West had managed to get him to agree to close down the digging and gather everyone together.

The next step had been harder, but she'd finally made him agree to go into town with Donovan and warn the sheriff of what was happening. Dr. Weiss had to be the one to do it—if only students went, Sheriff Gates might suspect a hoax.

Donovan was going along to make certain that a warning was given. Alyssa didn't trust Caitlin's father to stress the potential danger. He looked as if he wanted to go off and collect a few specimens for his museum.

"We have to get together for mutual protection," she explained to Donovan. "If you look at the way the jungle's growing, it seems to be forming a ring about us. If it closes in on us before we can get help, then we're going to be in serious trouble. If we aren't already."

"Maybe somebody should go for help?" Donovan suggested.

"We tried that, and were attacked," Alyssa pointed out. "Freeman's trying to get Denby to help us. I'd be willing to bet he's got a radio and everything we'll need to call for help. Maybe even a helicopter. With those guys, who knows? They've certainly got plenty of guns. So we can defend ourselves."

"*If* they'll help," Donovan pointed out. "They're not exactly all there in the head, you know. Who knows if they'll even believe Freeman?"

"They *have* to," Alyssa insisted. "Even they must have seen the dinosaurs by now, and understand that they're trouble."

"We can hope," Donovan agreed.

Now, Alyssa stood, watching the car depart for Furnace. Donovan had promised to check and see how the forest was growing in town. Maybe there was a way out there that wouldn't take them too close to the trees. Another run for help could work, in that case.

She turned to go and check up on Caitlin. She was worried about her friend. Caitlin had been acting oddly all day, and Alyssa was worried that she'd taken sick with some mutant bug. She saw Dr. West hurrying to meet her.

"Caitlin's gone," she announced abruptly. "I don't know where, or whether it was under her own steam. There's nothing to indicate that she's been kidnapped or attacked."

"Gone?" Alyssa felt a dull pain in the chest. This was another worry that they didn't need. "I thought she was supposed to be sleeping?"

"She was," Dr. West agreed. "Maybe some of the students could look for her. She can't have gotten far on her own, and if somebody took her, there might be signs. I'll organize a search party."

"Okay." Alyssa felt weary, totally drained. She was getting numbed to shocks.

As Dr. West hurried off, she heard the sound of an approaching motor. Shielding her eyes against the sun, she made out the humvee approaching.

Freeman jumped out as soon as it stopped. "The colonel didn't believe me," he reported glumly. "He thinks this is a trap to lure everyone out so they can be captured or killed."

"Damn his stupid paranoia," snarled Alyssa, really fed up. "We could have done with his help, Freeman. This is likely to get dangerous."

He managed a slight grin. "I've . . . borrowed some weapons that might help," he informed her.

A ray of hope, at least! "Bless you," she said sincerely. "So, you don't think this is a trap, then?"

"I can't believe you'd do anything like that," Freeman told her. "You're not the Mata Hari type."

"Oh, I don't know," she replied, managing to dredge some humor up from somewhere. "I might surprise you sometime." He blushed, and she smiled. "Don't worry," she assured him. "Now isn't one of those times. Right now, I just feel like trying to stay alive."

Freeman showed her what he'd brought. "You'd better see if anyone here has ever handled guns before," he told her. "I wouldn't want to give them to untrained people. They might do worse damage with them than the dinosaurs would."

"Makes sense," Alyssa agreed. "They might shoot us instead of their targets." *Why me?* she wondered. Why was everyone treating her as if she were the boss? Why not Dr. West, or Dr. Weiss? Well, okay, Dr. Weiss wasn't here, but Dr. West was. On the other hand, the scientist wasn't one for taking charge; she preferred to stay in the background and do her work. Alyssa was one of those natural-born organizers, and somehow people seemed to see this and simply take it for granted she'd get things done.

She and Freeman checked with the students, getting them together. Three of them had experience hunting, so Freeman gave each of them rifles and boxes of ammo. "Guard duty," Alyssa informed them. "We'll all stay around the main tents, so there's less ground to cover. You three take watch in turns. An hour on, an hour off. Have someone with you at all times. If you even *see* a dinosaur, alert everyone. Then feel free to try and kill the damned thing."

Chelsea Hoover, a graduate student, scowled. "Look, kid," she said, annoyed. "Some of us believe in conservation, you know. *If* there are dinosaurs around, we should be looking to protect them, not kill them."

Alyssa gave her a sweet smile. "I'm into conservation, too," she replied. "I'm conserving our lives. We can protect killer dinosaurs once we're safe. But I'll bear in mind that you're the first volunteer to be eaten." Ignoring her, she turned to Freeman. "Have I forgotten anything yet?"

"No," he answered, obviously impressed. "But it might

be an idea to see how much food and water there is in camp. We don't know how long we could be here.''

"That's something for you to do," Alyssa told Chelsea.

"Who made you boss?" Chelsea demanded. "You're just a kid and don't have any authority over us.''

"*I* say she's boss," Freeman said evenly. "And I think if you ask around all the others will agree." Chelsea glanced around and saw that everyone was nodding in support.

"Fine," she snapped, then hurried away. Alyssa hoped she was going to do the inventory, as she'd been asked.

"Right," Alyssa muttered. "What's next? Medical supplies." She hurried over to Dr. West's tent. They might need an awful lot of bandages and stuff before this thing was over.

Inside the tent, Dr. West was examining the last of the eggs. Alyssa was disturbed by this. "Are you sure that thing's safe?" she asked.

"I think so," Dr. West replied. "But it's fascinating. Somehow, it's losing mass."

"Come again?" Alyssa asked. Why couldn't the woman simply speak English?

"The stone seems to be somehow evaporating," Dr. West explained. "Remember, those other eggs were a lot thinner than this one? Well, when they're exposed to the air, somehow the stone sheathing about them seems to simply start evaporating. And once the egg is thin enough, I think it breaks open."

Alyssa could hardly believe what she was hearing and seeing. "Then don't you think it's kind of dumb to leave that out in the air?" she demanded. "Whatever's going on around here had to have been started by breaking open the first egg. I *really* think you should put that away somewhere airtight."

Dr. West blinked and looked down at it on her table as if the thought had never occurred to her. It probably hadn't. "You have a point," she admitted. "I'll put it back in the safe. That's airtight." Gently, she lifted up the egg, and walked across the tent with it.

As she stooped to replace it in the safe, there was a loud cracking sound. The egg simply fell to pieces in Dr. West's hand.

Alyssa tensed, expecting something to leap out. Instead, a small, greenish cloud formed, and almost immediately dissipated. Dr. West gave a shocked intake of breath and then collapsed. Instinctively, Alyssa started forward to go to the woman's aid, but Freeman grabbed her arm and held her back.

"No!" he exclaimed. "That was some kind of gas, or bacterial weapon! If you get closer, it'll get you, too." He sniffed, gingerly. "We'd best seal off the tent until we can be sure it's gone."

Alyssa pointed at Dr. West, stretched out on the ground. "She could be dying!" she protested, worried and scared.

"And so could you if you try and help her," Freeman said brutally. "I've got rebreather equipment in the humvee. I'll use it to get her out. But you stay far back, and keep everyone else away." He hurried off.

Standing in the doorway to the tent, Alyssa peered at Dr. West. She was pretty certain she could make out the rise and fall of her chest, so she wasn't dead. That was a great relief. But what had happened to her? And what had been in that egg? Some kind of gas?

Maybe the eggs were some sort of natural phenomenon? She'd heard that rock could be formed in volcanoes, and so could gases. Was it possible that the eggs were some sort of natural gas container? It simply didn't seem possible to her. So what else could it be? Caitlin had said very firmly that nothing could have lived for sixty million years encased in rock. On the other hand, the dinosaurs and the forest had to be coming from somewhere. Still, there had been nothing inside the rock container even vaguely like a dinosaur or a tree.

Seeds? Was it possible that the tiny cloud had been composed of seeds? That made a sort of sense, except it didn't explain living creatures, just plants.

Whatever was going on here, it was beyond her powers to figure out.

Freeman returned, his face covered by gas mask of some sophisticated design. He paused beside her. "That . . . egg . . . was millions of years old, right?" he asked, his voice distorted but recognizable.

"Right," she agreed.

"I just hope whatever was in it won't be absorbed through my skin," he said. "I don't have a biohazard suit."

"I'm amazed," Alyssa said drily. "I thought you guys had everything."

"Back at the farm," he said, missing her sarcasm. "It never occurred to me that we might need one."

It figured. She watched as he carefully crossed to Dr. West, and crouched down. He felt for the pulse on her neck, and then flashed Alyssa a thumbs-up sign to let her know the doctor was okay. Then he heaved her onto his shoulders, and walked out of the tent with her.

"Her pulse is strong," Freeman said, halting next to her. "Maybe she was only knocked out. Where shall I take her?"

"The sleeping tent," Alyssa decided. "Come on." She led the way to the girls' tent, and Freeman gently lowered Dr. West onto her bed. Alyssa removed the scientist's shoes, and covered her with a light sheet. "I'll see if anyone has any nursing training," she decided, as Freeman removed his mask. "Someone had better stay with her. We've lost one patient today."

"Lost?" Freeman looked worried. "You've had a death already?"

"No, she's just lost," Alyssa replied. "It's Caitlin. She either walked off, or somebody took her. We don't know."

"You're holding up well under all this pressure," Freeman said admiringly.

"That's because I haven't had a chance to scream and faint yet," Alyssa informed him. "It's one thing after another, so I guess the shock hasn't set in yet. You want to check on our guards, and I'll see if someone can look after the doctor."

"Right."

To Alyssa's surprise, Chelsea had finished inventorying the supplies. They had food for a week, but water only for a day or so. "And that's assuming we don't shower or use water in the toilet," Chelsea added. "It would be nice if we could get more."

"It would have to be from town," Alyssa replied. "I wouldn't dare touch the pond water in the forest. God knows what's in it."

It turned out that Chelsea had a little nursing experience. She'd volunteered the previous summer in a hospital. Quite the socially conscious activist, obviously, but Alyssa was grateful for it. Chelsea went off without a murmur to keep an eye on Dr. West.

Freeman returned, looking tired. "Well, they do seem to be on the ball," he told her, reporting on the guards. "As far as we can be, we're in good shape."

Alyssa nodded, staring at the surrounding jungle. It was so extensive now that it was difficult to see if it were spreading or not. She simply assumed it had to be. There didn't seem to be any limits to its growth yet.

"Maybe we should try making a break for it in the hum-vee?" Freeman suggested. "It's pretty tough, and even one of those dinosaurs couldn't make much of an impact on it."

"It's worth a try," Alyssa agreed. "We'd better wait for Dr. Weiss to return, though, before we try it. We need someone in charge." She simply assumed that he meant for the two of them to make the attempt together. She realized that she was getting to be quite dependent on him. He seemed to finally have put his brain into gear and wasn't simply accepting everything he was being told as the truth. He was turning out to be quite a guy. Maybe, when all of this was over, there might be . . .

She lost that train of thought as the sound of gunshots reached them. For a moment, she was too surprised to react. It wasn't their sentries; the noise was too far off. It wasn't the survivalists, either: the shooting was coming from the direction of Furnace. Her eyes locked with Freeman's.

"Trouble," he said. "I'll go and see what's happening."

"*We'll* go," Alyssa insisted. He didn't bother arguing, probably realizing he'd lose. They both jumped into the vehicle. "We'll be back!" she yelled at the student stand-ing sentry. "Watch out for trouble!" Then Freeman had the humvee racing.

It took them only about seven minutes to get to town, but they were the longest seven minutes of Alyssa's life. Her stomach was twisting itself into pretzel knots as they drew closer. The jungle was easily visible on the far side of the buildings now, and she realized with a shock that it formed almost a complete circle now, enclosing both the camp and the town. It looked like the only way out now was likely to be through the jungle . . .

Firing had continued as they approached. Alyssa began to see why as they reached the first house. With a shock, she realized that there were dinosaurs everywhere. There were several *Deinonychus,* along with dozens of smaller creatures that darted in and out of ferns that had started growing along the streets. There were others with what looked to be huge skulls, and some with armor and spiked-ball tails. There were a number of horned dinosaurs, and even a couple of quite colossal ones. Alyssa didn't have the vaguest idea what any of these might be called.

But she could see quite clearly what they were doing. They had surrounded Chaney's store, and were attacking everyone inside. It was from the store windows that the gunfire was issuing. Alyssa and Freeman exchanged worried looks.

The dinosaurs looked like they'd declared full-scale war on the humans in Furnace.

CHAPTER 10

"WE'VE GOT TO do something," Freeman said grimly, pausing the humvee at a safe distance. "I can see the sheriff's car and Dr. Weiss's there. If we can give them a chance, maybe they can run for it."

"Freeman," Alyssa pointed out, on the verge of panic, "if they get out of town, we only have *tents*. They won't stop an attack like this."

"Neither will the buildings here," he told her, pointing.

One of the larger dinosaurs—it was over eighteen feet tall, and looked like what she'd grown up calling a brontosaurus—had ambled slowly up to one of the houses. Rearing very slightly, it stomped down with its immense front feet. The deck, siding and one wall of the house simply collapsed under the assault. The monster then slammed its body against what was still standing.

A man ran from the house, carrying a hunting rifle but unable to use it. He tried to zigzag, but he didn't stand a chance. Alyssa gasped as about a dozen of the foot-high dinosaurs converged on the man and all leapt on him at once. He went down as they nipped at him. She wanted to be sick, but couldn't tear her gaze away.

Then, astonishingly, the dinosaurs all scurried away. The man sat up, shaking and bleeding, but as stunned to be alive as Alyssa was to see him still breathing. Once again, the creatures had attacked and not killed. It didn't make sense. Still, there was no guarantee that the others would be so lenient.

"Take the wheel," Freeman ordered. He slipped into the back, and opened his box of hand grenades. "I hope you can drive."

"I've got my learners permit," Alyssa confessed. "But haven't practiced driving through herds of dinosaurs."

"Well, now's your chance to make up for that staggering oversight," he answered with a grin. "And you don't even get penalized if you hit any. Just drive us past the store, and let me do the rest, okay?"

"That I can manage." She slid into the driver's seat and gunned the engine. "Here we go."

Her driving would certainly have made her fail back home. She overrevved the engine, almost slipped the clutch and she was shaking so hard that it was a wonder the vehicle ran in the direction she intended. But she kept it on track, ignoring anything that was in her way. The humvee flattened a couple of the midsized dinosaurs before she decided to veer to avoid one of the armor-plated kind. She was pretty sure the humvee would do more damage to it than it could do to them, but there was no point in taking chances.

Freeman leaned out of the side window, and started lobbing grenades. The dinosaurs obviously didn't know what to make of these, and they simply ignored them.

The first one exploded under one of the armored dinosaurs. Alyssa didn't look, but there was a rain of blood and squishy things she didn't want to examine. One after another, the grenades exploded. Animal screams punctuated the blasts.

One of the *Deinonychus* monsters tried jumping them in the car. Freeman whipped his hand inside, and the thing managed only a thin score along his arm, leaving a trail of blood. Freeman dropped a grenade into the creature's mouth. "Bite this, sucker," he snarled. A moment later, there was another explosion behind them, and another rain of blood. Alyssa wasn't normally a vicious person, but she was really glad they were managing to kill some of these things.

"Slow down in front of the store," Freeman ordered. He was ignoring the graze he'd received, and was readying more grenades. "We've got to give the survivors a chance to make the cars."

"Right," she agreed, stepping on the brake. Chaney's was close now, but they had broken through the dinosaur horde. Freeman lobbed more grenades. As they exploded, Alyssa swung the humvee in an arc, taking out a couple more of the things as she did so.

From the corner of her eye, she saw people hurrying to the cars, firing whatever weapons they had as they ran. There didn't seem to be very many people left, and she was concentrating too hard on driving to see who they might be. The brontosauruslike monster was leaving off flattening houses and heading in their direction now. Alyssa didn't like that; even a grenade might not stop a monster like that. . . .

The two cars were crammed, and both started up. The dinosaurs started to converge on them now, abandoning the attack on the store. Freeman threw more grenades, trying to clear a path for the escapees, but then he came up empty in the box. "Easy come, easy go," he muttered. He pulled a machine gun from the backseat, and started laying down fire with that next.

Alyssa was starting to go deaf from all the noise. It rang inside the humvee, and was hurting her head. Freeman yelled something, but she couldn't make out the words. She hoped it was "get us out of here," and acted accordingly. A few more smaller dinosaurs died as she ran them down. Another *Deinonychus* tried to get the vehicle, but Freeman brought it crashing down with the machine gun.

Then they were free of the attackers, and heading into the desert behind the two cars. Alyssa put the pedal to the floor and clutched the steering wheel for dear life. Freeman stopped firing, but cradled his smoking gun, watching back the way they had come.

Somehow or other, the drive back seemed to be less than seven minutes. Shaking, Alyssa pulled the humvee as close to the tents as she could before stopping it. She had to sit still, bent over the wheel, breathing heavily for a few moments before she dared try standing up. Freeman leaned across and kissed her on the cheek. "You just passed my driving test," he told her. "Battle ready, that's you."

"Scared spitless, that's me," Alyssa confessed. She managed to get out of the transport without falling over. There were splashes of blood and internal organs all over the front of the humvee, but she didn't care. She staggered rather than walked over to the knot of new arrivals.

Dr. Weiss and Donovan were there, along with Sheriff Gates, Chaney, the town doctor, the man who'd been attacked in the street and a couple of women. "This is it?" Alyssa asked, appalled. "Nobody else made it?"

Sheriff Gates shook his head. "A whole lot of people seem to have just vanished," he told her. "Before the attack came. When Dr. Weiss warned us, we rounded up everyone we could find, and assembled at Chaney's store. Then the things came out of nowhere and started attacking us." He glanced at Freeman. "Glad you came along, son. You sure made them pause and think. But where's the rest of your men?"

"They didn't come with me," Freeman answered. "But they must have heard the noise. I imagine they'll be investigating soon."

Weariness now overtook Alyssa. "I've got to rest," she said. "I can't go on any longer." Sunset was just starting. "Freeman, let me sleep for an hour, or I'll be useless."

"No problem," he assured her. "Get some rest. You've earned it."

Alyssa staggered to her sleeping tent. Dr. West was still there, sleeping. Chelsea nodded to Alyssa, but didn't say anything. Shaking all over, Alyssa collapsed onto her bed. All she could see when she closed her eyes were dinosaur's leaping at her. . . . Still, somehow, she fell asleep.

It was much darker when she awoke. Checking her watch, she saw that it was almost one in the morning. She'd been out for about five hours. Freeman had ignored her orders. Still, she was kind of glad, because at least she felt a little better now. She sat up, running a hand through her hair. It felt damp and really in need of a good wash, but there was neither the time nor the water for that.

The town doctor was sitting with Dr. West. He gave Alyssa a thin smile as she walked over to him. "How's she doing?" Alyssa asked.

"Superficially, quite well," he replied. "She's almost comatose, though, and I don't know quite what's happening to her body."

"What do you mean?" Alyssa asked, alarmed.

The doctor had a small flashlight, which he focused on

a patch of skin on Dr. West's neck. Alyssa felt like gagging. The skin was bumpy, like a really bad rash. It was also greenish in color.

"Infected?" she gasped.

"No infection I've ever seen before," the doctor answered. "Dr. Weiss and I have been running some tests, though. There's something in her blood that's attacking her body."

"Is she going to die?" Alyssa asked, pained. She liked Dr. West.

"I don't think she'll be that lucky," the doctor answered enigmatically. "Freeman tells me that she breathed in some kind of dust or virus. Whatever it was has invaded her body. It's changing her metabolism somehow. I took blood samples, and they show the strangest results."

Alyssa didn't like the sound of any of that. "I'd better talk to Dr. Weiss," she said. "Is he still awake?"

The doctor nodded. "He and the sheriff are in the work tent."

"No more dinosaur attacks?" she asked.

"No." The doctor shrugged. "I understand that dinosaurs are lizards, and so cold-blooded. They're not able to move at night, in that case. We should be safe until after sunrise."

"There's a cheery thought." Alyssa left the tent and headed for the work tent. She saw that there were three people on guard duty, all armed. One of them was Freeman, who saluted her with gentle irony. Didn't he ever need sleep?

Dr. Weiss looked up as she entered the tent. "Ah, Alyssa. Feeling better?"

"As well as you can feel when you're under assault by creatures that seem to have forgotten they've been dead sixty million years."

"Quite." He looked almost happy, oddly enough. "But I've been piecing together what's happened. Dr. West's infection has been most helpful in that regard."

"*Helpful*?" Alyssa couldn't believe the callousness of that comment.

"Yes." If he caught her shock and pain, he gave no sign. "It seems that you must have been partially correct in thinking that those egg-stones contained dinosaur embryos. In fact, they contained some sort of viral agent. It seems to be astonishingly adaptive. It enters any kind of living organism and then restructures it. It somehow transforms the DNA of the host into something else. The sheriff tells me that the first disappearances were of cats and dogs. The virus must have transformed them into small dinosaurs. Then other creatures were infected. It's astonishingly fecund."

"It's infecting *people*," Alyssa pointed out. She turned to the sheriff. "This must be why those people vanished."

"Yeah, I'd kind of got that far myself," Sheriff Gates agreed. "It looks like some of the monsters we killed might once have been my neighbors." He looked disturbed by the thought. "But what I want to know is if there's a way to make the rest of us immune. Or if there's a cure we can use on anyone who's infected."

"A cure?" Dr. Weiss shrugged. "Out here, with no resources? No. In a well-equipped lab or hospital? Possibly. And I can't think of any way to protect us from the virus. If it infects us, we're doomed."

"You don't sound too put-out by that," the sheriff objected.

"This is a fascinating opportunity for a scientist," Dr. Weiss replied. "We're seeing the rebirth of species dead for millions of years. I'm too excited to be worried."

"Then start wondering how you're going to write your

reports and scientific papers when you're a *Deinonychus*,''
Alyssa snapped. She turned to the sheriff. ''We've got to
get out of here as soon as we can,'' she said. ''I couldn't
tell if the jungle formed a complete ring or not yet, but if
we wait here, we'll all be infected sooner or later. Can we
make a break for it tonight?''

''Driving across the desert in the dark?'' The sheriff
shook his head. ''Too dangerous, especially if the jungle's
closed in. I'd sooner wait for first light, when we can see
obstructions.''

''We can't wait any longer than that,'' Alyssa said
firmly. ''As soon as it gets warm, those monsters will be
on the move again.'' She glanced at Dr. Weiss. ''How long
do you think that will give us?''

''An hour after sunrise,'' he said. ''Maybe two.''

''Then we have to have everyone ready to move just as
the sun peeks out,'' Alyssa decided. She still couldn't believe that she was the one making decisions here. Dr. Weiss
was too far out of reality to be any use, she knew, but surely
the sheriff should be running things? Then she saw the
relief on his face, and realized that he was simply completely out of his depth here. Tracking criminals, patrolling
the town and arresting drunks were his kind of work. This
was just too much for him.

Well, it was too much for her, too, but it had to be done.

''There's another small problem,'' the sheriff confessed.
''We've got more people here than will fit into the vehicles,
even cramming them like sardines. We're going to have to
leave at least six people behind.''

Six people . . . Alyssa was shocked. She simply hadn't
thought about that. But she couldn't abandon anyone here,
to be killed. Or worse, be turned into a dinosaur. There *had*
to be something they could do. ''I'll work something out,''
she promised vaguely, without any ideas.

Leaving the tent, she breathed in the cool air, and tried to make some sense out of what she'd been hearing. They had to escape, that was clear—*if* there was still a way out. What if the jungle had encircled them by now? And how could she plan on leaving six people behind? She didn't want to be the leader, and have to make that kind of decision.

She walked along the tents, and stood outside the girl's sleeping tent. Everyone not on watch was resting, which was good. At least they'd all be in some shape to travel in the morning. All but six of them . . .

"Alyssa?"

Stiffening at the sound of the voice, Alyssa whirled around. There was a shadowy figure beside the tent, and she recognized that voice. "Caitlin?" she asked, incredulous. She had almost forgotten about her missing friend, what with everything else. "Caitlin! Are you all right?"

"No," Caitlin answered. "I'm not. But there's nothing you or anyone can do about it now."

Alyssa moved forward. "What's wrong?" she asked, solicitously. "Let me help."

"No!" Caitlin pulled back. "Alyssa, stay away from me. I . . . don't know if I can control myself."

"What are you talking about?" Alyssa asked, concerned. Maybe she was still delirious? "Come on, let us help you."

"I'm fighting it," Caitlin said, her voice strange and agonized. "But it's so hard, and I know I'm not going to win. Alyssa you've got to get out of here."

"We're going in the morning," Alyssa promised, trying to move in closer. "You'll be coming with us."

"No," her friend said. "Not anymore. I don't belong with you anymore. Not in the human world."

"What are you talking about?" Alyssa demanded, scared. *Oh, God!* Caitlin had been infected. . . . But she wasn't a dinosaur, because she could still talk. It didn't make any sense.

Then Caitlin moved into a small pool of light. Alyssa wanted to scream.

It was Caitlin, and it wasn't. There were bits of Caitlin left. . . .

Her body was mostly green, and slightly scaled. Her clothes were gone, but she didn't need them any longer. Tufts of her bright red hair remained, but she was mostly bald. Her head was more egg-shaped, the nose mere slits in her face. Her eyes were larger and almost completely black. There was a slight ridge across her skull, and running down what she could see of Caitlin's back. Her fingers were longer and thinner.

"I'm not human anymore," Caitlin breathed.

CHAPTER 11

"CAITLIN!" ALYSSA BREATHED, trying not to feel revolted. "What's happened to you?"

"Change," Caitlin answered. "It's what the *dainid* intended."

"But it's still you inside?" Alyssa asked, uncertainly.

"All of me is still here," Caitlin replied. "But there's somebody else with me now. I have to try and explain to you, Alyssa. Please don't be disgusted!"

"I'm not," Alyssa told her, and found that she was only half-lying. It seemed that, although very different in appearance, this was still her best friend. "We can't stay out here," she added. "The sentries might spot you, and they're not likely to be very glad to see you."

The creature that was partly Caitlin nodded. "The supply tent," she suggested. "Only, Alyssa—don't get too close to me. I'm fighting the instincts as hard as I can. But I *really* want to scratch you.''

Alyssa frowned. ''Whatever for?''

''To infect you with the virus that's doing all of this,'' Caitlin explained. ''It's part of my purpose. But I don't want to do this to you. Unless you *want* it.''

Alyssa couldn't repress a shudder at that thought. ''Thanks, but I think I'd rather keep my hair.''

Caitlin touched her few remaining strands, which were still being shed. ''Yes. I miss that.'' Then she turned and made her way to the supply tent. Alyssa followed, and slipped inside. Caitlin was at the far end of the tent, huddled in shadows. She was obviously very sensitive about her appearance.

''What did you want to talk to me about?'' Alyssa asked gently.

''I have to tell you what's happening,'' Caitlin answered. ''You've got to get the rest of the humans out of here, or you'll all end up like me. I can hold the others off for a while, but it's not so easy with the more primitive ones. They'll attack again in the morning.''

It was finally starting to make some sense to Alyssa. ''The virus was inside the eggs,'' she said, remembering what Dr. Weiss had worked out. ''It invades the body through the cell membranes—if you're cut, or breath it directly in, like Dr. West.''

''Yes,'' Caitlin confirmed. ''It's designed to alter the native DNA of the host organism and then alter it to dinosaur DNA, the closest equivalent. It's part of an incredible survival plan dating back sixty million years. . . .

''Alyssa, I now have memories from that time, and I know what's happening and why. There was a species of dinosaur that we've not yet discovered. A very evolved species with intelligence as great as humans. They were called the *dainid*.'' She gestured at herself. ''This is how they looked. They evolved into an intelligent society, but along very different lines than human society.

''But then came the comet. The theories were right about a comet striking the earth and wiping out the dinosaurs. The explosion and the dust it kicked up sent the earth into a deep ice age that killed so many species. The *dainid* knew that this was going to happen, but they couldn't escape. They didn't have space travel, or any way of surviving the terrible cold that would come. But they had developed their knowledge of biology.

''They created the virus, and sealed it inside stone containers. It was a brilliant idea. The stones would only open in the presence of sufficient temperature and moisture for them to survive. The virus would then infect whatever life survived the comet's impact, and the *dainid* would live again. In fact, they created what amounted to a Noah's Ark of DNAs. Enough to recreate all of the creatures and plant life they would need to survive. The stones were buried deep inside flows of lava and dust. Unfortunately, instead of rising to the surface in a few thousand years as was planned, they were buried for sixty million years. We— *they*—never imagined that another intelligent species would evolve upon the earth before they could be reborn. Another species that could . . . threaten their own.

''Believe me, Alyssa, the *dainid* part of me is appalled that the Caitlin part of me has been absorbed. They are a very peaceful species, and this is abhorrent to them. But what could they—*we*—do? Alyssa, it's exhilarating! I'm so much stronger, faster and more intelligent than I ever was. It's wonderful.''

''Maybe,'' Alyssa said. ''But you're sure going to have a problem getting a date for the prom, looking like that.''

Caitlin grunted a laugh. ''Human dates, perhaps. But to

a *dainid* male, this is a very alluring body. And there now are *dainid* males. Many of the townsfolk were infected.''

Something suddenly occurred to Alyssa. ''Freeman was scratched.''

''Then he's going to become one of us, too,'' Caitlin said simply. ''It's inevitable. He's no longer human, whatever he looks like.'' She sounded wistful. ''I imagine he'll make a strong *dainid* male . . .''

It was horrible to even contemplate, but Alyssa forced herself to think straight. ''Anyone who's been scratched is infected?''

''Yes.'' Caitlin nodded. ''That's why the *Deinonychus* didn't kill me when it was hunting for food. It could smell that I was one of its own kind, and spared me.'' She shrugged, a very human gesture for a creature that looked so alien. ''They're not very bright, but they're good hunting companions. We'll try and keep them in line, but it's not very easy.''

''What do you mean?'' Alyssa wasn't following her friend. Perhaps it was just that she was tired, or that Caitlin wasn't thinking like a human any longer.

''We will try to let you go tomorrow,'' Caitlin answered. ''We have been talking, and we know it's wrong to force you to change if you don't wish it. There are enough of us now to begin a breeding colony, so we don't really *need* more humans to convert.''

''*Try* to let us go?'' Alyssa repeated, worried.

''It's not that simple.'' Caitlin looked pained. ''What I *really* want to do now, programmed by the virus, is to slash your skin and make you one of us. I really want you to be with us, not just because that's the instinct, but because I know I'll miss you dreadfully if you go. But, at the same time, I know how revolted you must feel by the idea, and

I don't want to force you to change. You'd have to *want* it.'' She sounded wistful again.

Alyssa shuddered. She could accept that this creature was her friend, but there was no way she would ever want to end up like that . . . Maybe she'd feel different if she were changed, but she didn't want to feel different. She liked being herself. ''I'm afraid I'm in favor of getting out of here,'' she admitted. ''So, you're going to let us go?''

''We'll *try*,'' Caitlin said. ''The problem is that the an-imals—the smaller dinosaurs—can't keep their program-ming in check. They may attack you even if we tell them not to. It won't be simple. They have this burning desire to scratch . . .'' Caitlin's fingers suddenly opened to reveal long claws. She shuddered, and managed to retract them. ''It's very hard to control. I'm going to have to leave soon, because the urge to attack is very strong. But you must explain this to the rest of the humans. Tell them to be ready in the morning. We will escort you through the jungle.''

''The paths out have all closed up?'' Alyssa asked.

''By the morning, they will have,'' Caitlin confirmed. ''The jungle is growing as it was intended.''

Alyssa shivered at the thought. ''Caitlin, what's the point in leaving?'' she asked, filled with bitterness suddenly. ''The jungle is still growing. The dinosaurs will infect any-one they scratch. Even if we leave, you're going to be ex-panding. It's bound to touch another town somewhere, and this will start again.''

''We know,'' Caitlin said. ''We are trying to do some-thing about it.''

''And someone in authority is going to see what's hap-pening,'' Alyssa realized. ''They're going to figure out what's causing it. And they're going to try and stop it. Cait, you *know* what that means! They're going to try and de-stroy you!''

"Yes," agreed Caitlin sadly. "They will try. We have a plan, that may work. But we will worry about that later. The first thing to do is to get you all to safety. You *must* go with us when we come to you. And, whatever you do, don't start any killing. If the animals smell blood, their instincts will overwhelm our control. Please, Caitlin, you *must* convince the others of this." She sighed. "Though I imagine you'll have trouble with my father. He's very stubborn."

Alyssa nodded. The weird thing was that she had already stopped shuddering at Caitlin's appearance. She was still Caitlin, whatever she looked like. She was still her friend. "Okay, I'll do what I can."

Caitlin nodded. "There's one last thing," she added. "Denby's group."

"Aren't they outside the jungle?" asked Alyssa, surprised.

"No. They followed Freeman here, and they're sitting outside in the darkness. They seem to think this is a big trap to catch them." Caitlin laughed. "In one sense, they're right. They just think it's the government, not the *dainid*. But they're ready to start shooting. You have to convince them to join with you."

Alyssa groaned. "And what do I do for an encore?" she asked. "Part the Red Sea? Cait, those guys won't listen to me."

"They will if you do it right," Caitlin insisted. "I can point you in the right direction, and make sure you get there safely."

"Why me?" Alyssa complained. Then she sighed. "Okay. I'd better do it before I get smart and refuse." She walked to the tent flap. "Which way?"

Caitlin came to stand beside her, and pointed to the south. "That way. Straight out, about a mile."

Alyssa turned to look at her friend. The large, dark eyes stared back at her. "Caitlin, take care," she whispered. "Whatever you look like, you'll always be my friend."

"And you mine," Caitlin answered, somewhat tensely. She was screwing her fists tight. "Go, now, before I lose control."

Taking the warning, Alyssa headed out of the tent and out of the camp. She marched straight ahead, trying hard not to think of what might be lurking in the darkness. If the dinosaurs were cold-blooded, they should be sleeping the night away. But Caitlin hadn't been sleeping, and when she had stood next to Alyssa, there had been warmth from her body. If the *dainid* were warm-blooded, like humans, then perhaps some of the other dinosaurs were, too. And they might be out there now. . . .

Alyssa stumbled along in the darkness, wondering how far she had gone. She could see the lay of the land, though not very well. There was no moon, and the starlight, though clear, was not very bright. Finally, though, she saw a shape in the night that looked more human than dinosaur. "Hey!" she called. "You wouldn't happen to have a cup of sugar I could borrow, would you?"

The unamused guard took her in to see Denby. Alyssa wasn't surprised to find him awake, and he was trying hard not to look like he was surprised that she had found them.

"What do you want?" he demanded roughly. "Are you crazy, coming out alone and unarmed at night?"

"Probably," Alyssa answered. "I came to try and save your lives."

That got his attention, as she'd hoped. "You're warning me of a trap? The government is waiting?"

"Yes and no." Alyssa knew her best bet was to phrase this in terms he could understand and accept. "There's a trap, but it's not the government. It's intelligent dinosaurs."

He raised an eyebrow. "Isn't that a contradiction in terms?"

Yes, like intelligent militia, she thought. "I thought so, too, until a short while back. But I ran into one. They were planning on killing everyone, but I managed to negotiate a deal. They didn't know you were here, and thought we humans were defenseless. But your presence changed the whole thing, and they're willing to give us safe passage out of here as long as we don't start fighting them."

Denby raised an eyebrow. "Very decent of them."

"It's the best offer we're going to get," she snapped. "It's either that, or else get picked off by dinosaurs."

Denby shook his head. "They can't get my men; they're too well trained."

"Really?" Alyssa decided it was time to bluff a little, and hoped she could pull it off. "And how many sentries do you have out now?"

"Two."

"I only saw one," she answered. "Are you *sure* there's two?"

For the first time, Denby looked uncertain. "Semanski!" he yelled. When one of his men appeared, he snapped: "Check on Corman." Semanski saluted and left. Denby regarded Alyssa with concern. "What is it that you propose?"

"Come to our camp, and join with us," she said. "We have an escort leaving in the morning. We can escape this trap together."

"If your offer isn't the trap," Denby countered.

Alyssa sighed. "Doesn't your paranoia ever get a rest? Look, do I seem to be smart enough to be able to fool you? I'm just a school kid, trying to stay alive. We've got a better chance together than we have apart, that's all."

She could see that she'd made a good point there. He

was still mulling it over when Semanski returned. "Couldn't find Corman, sir," he barked. "He's no longer at his post."

Alyssa smiled. "Still think your men can take on anything?" she asked.

After a moment, he looked at her again. "You're proposing a truce?" he suggested. "Until we get away from the dinosaurs?"

"Right."

Denby nodded. "Very well. We'll come to your camp at first light." He held up a hand. "But at the first sign of trouble, we'll start shooting."

Marvelous! thought Alyssa sarcastically. What an arrangement. "Agreed," she said. "Well, see you in the morning."

"Do you want an escort back?" Denby asked. Alyssa realized he was actually being nice, but she couldn't help herself.

"I wouldn't want to lose him," she said sweetly. "I think we'll all be safer if I go alone." Then, with a feeling of immense satisfaction, she turned and walked off into the night. She'd have felt a lot happier about it if she hadn't immediately stubbed her toe on a rock. *Some heroine you are,* she thought, wincing. Hoping Caitlin was still watching out for her, she headed back toward the camp.

CHAPTER 12

SOMEHOW, ALYSSA MANAGED to get a little more rest, but her eyes were open as the new day began. She had slept in her clothes, and simply rolled out of bed. Chelsea was already awake, and the two of them went about shaking the others. Dr. West was awake again, pale and shaken. Alyssa didn't look forward to having to tell her what she knew, but somebody was going to have to tell the woman that she wasn't human any longer. She still looked it, but it was only a matter of time until the changes became obvious.

Silently, everyone gathered outside the laboratory tent. "Everybody" was the handful of students and the smaller handful of townsfolk. No more than thirty of them, and not all of them would be leaving. . . .

"Denby should be here any moment," Alyssa announced. "He and his men will be joining us on the march out."

"March?" the sheriff asked sharply. He gestured at the cars. "Aren't we taking the vehicles, like we planned?"

"Take a look out there," Alyssa suggested. Everyone did so, silently. The trees were all around them now, and closing in. "The jungle's too thick to drive through. We have to walk."

"We'll never make it," one of the townsmen gasped.

"We will," Alyssa said. There was a noise at the edge of the camp as Denby and his eight men arrived.

"We're all that's left," the colonel said grimly. "Four of my men have vanished. Now I think it's time to make plans."

Dr. Weiss nodded. "We have to get out of here and go for help. This place has to be preserved for study."

The sheriff stared at him, and then shook his head. "It's got to be bombed into nothing. The rate it's spreading, it'll infect the whole country in a matter of weeks."

Before the two men could argue further, Alyssa broke in. "The decision is no longer ours to make," she informed them. "It's the *dainid* who will decide."

"Who are these . . . *dainid*?" demanded Dr. Weiss.

"Intelligent dinosaurs," Alyssa replied. She explained to everyone what Caitlin had told her during the night. She winced as she was forced to tell them all that anyone who had been bitten was infected, and would have to stay. "That includes you, Freeman," she said sadly. "Dr. West, too. You're already on the way to becoming *dainid*."

Freeman looked like he was going to puke. "You can't mean it," he insisted.

"She does," said Caitlin. Her voice, from near the supply tent, made everyone turn. Denby half-raised his gun, but stopped himself.

Caitlin was now completely transformed. In the daylight, she looked sleek and fit, but so very alien. Alyssa wanted to weep for what Caitlin had lost, but her friend seemed to be self-assured and content. She glanced at Dr. Weiss, who had gone pale as he saw what had become of his daughter.

"I am a *dainid* now," Caitlin said gently. "Some of you will be, too. The rest of you must leave, before you become transformed. It is very urgent. We will escort you through the jungle safely." Other *dainid* emerged from the nearby trees, to stand with her.

"No," Denby said firmly, raising his rifle, but not actually targeting anyone. "This is a trick. They're going to take us off and then attack us when we're not expecting it."

"Paranoid as always," Caitlin said sadly. "If we wanted to attack you, we already would have. As soon as we could, we prevented the dinosaurs from coming after you. We have a measure of control over them, but it is very fragile. If you stay with us, you'll be safe. If you don't, we cannot guarantee you will not be attacked."

Dr. Weiss looked sick. "What has happened to you?" he asked her. "What have you done with my daughter?"

"I *am* your daughter," Caitlin insisted. "Merely . . . more now. I have the *dainid* consciousness added to me."

Sheriff Gates was disturbed. "We need time to think about your offer," he said. "You have to realize that this is a shock to us all."

"Yes," Caitlin agreed. "We will wait. But it would be better if you did not take too long. We want to get you out of here before the animals start hunting for the day." She and the other *dainid* withdrew to the edge of the forest.

"We can't trust them," Denby said firmly. "They're not human. They'll betray us, and attack us."

"Can't you trust *anyone*?" Alyssa demanded. "You're trapped in your own warped little world, where everyone is against you. Well, I've got news for you. You're not worth bothering about! The government isn't after you because you're not worth their time. We're not after you because we don't care about you. And the *dainid* aren't after you because they don't want to hurt anyone. Coming with us is your only chance of getting out of here alive. You'll have to decide whether that's important enough to you to take a risk on trusting somebody for a change.''

"She's right," Freeman agreed. "Colonel, with due respect, you're wrong."

Denby gave him a filthy look. "You're a traitor to the militia," he said with disgust. "You turned your back on us to throw your lot in with the enemy. And now you're being changed into one of *them*, so you're a traitor to the human race, too. I ought to put a bullet through your brain."

Freeman glared back at him. "You're sick," he said firmly. "You and reality aren't on speaking terms anymore." His shoulders sagged. "I know I have to stay, but I'll die before I let anything happen to the rest of you. I'm still human right now, and I'm on your side. So, I think, are the *dainid*."

Sheriff Gates sighed. "The question we have to face is . . . can we trust them?"

"I trust Caitlin," Alyssa replied. "I'm sure she's telling us the truth."

"That . . . *thing*, is not my daughter," Dr. Weiss said savagely. "My daughter is dead to me. That thing is some ancient creature, part of species that should have died out millions of years ago. They don't belong here, and should all be killed."

"That's the first sensible thing I've heard anyone say today," Denby agreed. "We have to kill these *dainid* before they kill us. They can only come about by infecting humans, so, whatever they claim, they've got to attack us to live.''

"No!" Alyssa insisted. "They're stable genetically. They can *breed*. They don't need any more human victims."

"Breed?" Dr. Weiss looked stunned. "They're viable?"

"Yes," Alyssa confirmed.

"Dear God, it's worse than I thought!" Dr. Weiss was pale and shaking. "This jungle area is still growing. These *dainid* are going to try and force the human race off this planet and reclaim it for themselves! We have a duty to the human race to stop them!"

"How?" asked Dr. West angrily. "By getting out and bombing this place? By killing them all?"

"Yes!" Dr. Weiss nodded violently. "It's our survival or theirs—and they lost their chance sixty million years ago."

"You'd kill your own daughter?" Dr. West demanded. "You'd kill *me*? I'm one of them now, or will be soon. What do you want to do, put a bullet through my heart?"

Dr. Weiss looked uncomfortable. "It's for the survival of the human race," he insisted. "This thing must be stopped."

"I'm not sure I'd want to be a part of your concept of the human race," Alyssa told him. "Caitlin said they're trying to stop the growth. They didn't know there would be intelligent beings here when this happened. They don't want to wipe us out."

"So those things say," Denby snapped. "But we can't trust them. I say we kill them all, starting with those of us here who are infected."

Freeman had his rifle covering the colonel. "I can't let you do that," he said, softly but firmly. "We have a right to life, as much as anyone. I'll help you all get out, but I won't let you kill me. Or the other *dainid*.''

Alyssa tried to defuse the situation. ''We have to make a decision!'' she cried. ''I'm going to trust them to keep their word. I'm going with them. Who else is with me?''

''I am,'' Chelsea announced, stepping forward.

''Me, too,'' agreed Donovan. One by one, most of the students and townspeople stepped forward. Hesitantly, Semanski left the ranks of the militia.

''I'll risk it,'' he agreed, not looking at the colonel. Five of the others followed him. The sheriff and the doctor both joined Alyssa.

There were two groups now left. Dr. West, Freeman and two of the townsfolk who'd been bitten stood together. They were all changing, and had to stay. The other group consisted of Denby, his two remaining men and Dr. Weiss.

''I'm not trusting them,'' Dr. Weiss announced. ''They've killed my daughter and others. I want them wiped out.''

Denby smiled nastily, and handed him a pistol. ''It looks like we're going to have to do this together,'' he said. ''We'll have to make a break for it. Once we're out, we'll wipe this place from the face of the map. We'll be the men who saved civilization.''

''You'll be dead,'' Alyssa said. ''Come with us . . . *please*!''

Denby just laughed, and turned to his small party. ''Come on.'' He set off toward the waiting jungle. His men and Dr. Weiss went with them without a backward glance.

Alyssa sighed. There was nothing more that they could do. She gestured to Caitlin to return. The *dainid* made their way into the camp again. ''We're going with you, Cait,'' Alyssa explained. ''Your father . . . refused to trust.''

''Then I'm sorry for him,'' Caitlin said gently. ''He

won't make it out. Now, come with us, all of you. We must hurry.''

The group moved together, the *dainid* on the edges, forming a barrier about them. Freeman carried his gun cradled in his arms, and walked next to Alyssa. They entered the jungle, and Caitlin led the way.

It was incredible. Only a few days ago, this had been nothing but desert. Now, the entire ecology had changed. There were trees, flowers, bushes everywhere. There were cries in the trees and from the tangle of forest, but only the occasional pteranodon was visible. The other dinosaurs were obeying the *dainid* and staying back.

As the sun rose higher, the forest was awakening about them. Alyssa could hear water running close by, and realized that somehow the *dainid* had brought a river back to the desert.

"How is all of this possible?" she asked Caitlin.

"We understand the sciences of life better than humans," she replied. "We can do things undreamed of by human technology. We will take care of this area, I promise you."

There were sounds of gunshots off in the direction Denby's party had taken. And then roaring of vast, ancient creatures. Alyssa glanced nervously from Caitlin to Freeman.

"They have been found," Caitlin said sadly. "They would not listen and trust."

The attack was over in moments. Dr. Weiss had seen very little other than snarling teeth. He had fired at everything until his gun was empty, screaming hysterically the whole time. Denby's men had been more thorough, mowing down the attacking dinosaurs. A *Deinonychus* had fallen, dead, barely a foot away from Dr. Weiss. He was soaked in its blood.

Denby had been ripped to shreds by two others. The two militiamen had fallen prey to a host of smaller dinosaurs that simply overran them. Dr. Weiss had turned and tried to flee. Six or seven of the smaller creatures had leaped him, but he had thrown them off.

To his shock, he was still alive. There were dinosaur corpses and the three human remains with him, but he was still alive. Giggling from the shock, he stumbled to his feet. His trousers were in shreds, where they had been ripped open.

Blood was trickling from several gashes in his legs where he had been bitten.

He went rigid and cold as he realized what this meant.

He was infected. . . .

In a matter of days, maybe only hours, he would cease being human. He would become *dainid*. . . .

No. He couldn't let that happen. They might have killed him slowly, but he wasn't going to allow them their victory. Shaking, but resolved, he crossed to the body of the closest militiaman. He still had his pistol in its holster. Nervously, Dr. Weiss pulled it out. There was one way he could prevent the *dainid* from completely defeating him. . . .

There was one final gunshot in the distance, and then silence.

Alyssa turned back to Caitlin. "They're dead," she said, with conviction.

"Yes," agreed Caitlin, sadly.

The hike went on. The jungle was clearly several miles thick now. Alyssa looked up at the sky, and frowned. It seemed to be taking on an odd sheen. Must be the humidity rising from the jungle, she supposed. But the light seemed awfully odd.

And as they drew closer to the edge of the jungle, the oddness grew more pronounced. It was like there was something in the sky. Caitlin caught her looking and wrinkled her nose. The way her face was constructed, she couldn't smile.

"It's our doing," she confirmed. "You'll see in a moment."

They came to the end of the jungle where the desert began again, and Alyssa did see. Rising from the ground, sweeping up overhead, was the start of some kind of a dome. It was enormous, the size of a large city. It looked to be made of ice or something. She stared at it, not understanding.

"Crystal," Caitlin explained. "We are growing it to enclose our domain. It will keep in the virus, until we can control it. The rest of the world will be safe from it. And we will be safe from the rest of the world. We shall seal ourselves in here."

"A prison?" asked Alyssa, concerned for her friend.

"A refuge," Caitlin replied. "For now. We must grow stronger. When the time is right, we will resume contact with the human race. Perhaps our children and yours. Until then, we must stay here, in order to be safe. It will take humans a long time to accept us and not want to kill us."

Alyssa nodded. "You're probably right. There are a lot of Denbys and Dr. Weisses out there." She looked sadly at her *dainid* friend. "I'll miss you, though."

"I'll miss you, too," Caitlin answered. Hesitantly, she hugged Alyssa. This time she didn't need to make her hands into fists to control her urges. "Take care."

"You too." Alyssa stepped through a small gap in the crystal, and the rest of the refugees followed her. Freeman and Dr. West remained within. Alyssa turned to wave good-bye, and saw that the crystal was already growing together, knitting to form the promised barrier.

"Do you think that the military will let them live?" she asked Donovan, who was next to her. "They might decide to nuke them." There was a catch in her throat at the thought.

"I don't think so," Donovan replied. "They can't be sure they'd destroy all of the virus. If they only broke the shield, it would spread, and then they'd never contain it. I think they'll go along with leaving the *dainid* alone." He put an arm about her shoulder. "Caitlin will be okay. Will you?"

"I guess," Alyssa answered. She leaned against him, glad for the company. Then she managed a slight grin. "Won't Doreen be mad at you for hugging me?"

"Daphne?" Donovan smiled. "Or is it Daisy?"

Alyssa laughed, glad of something to relieve the stress. "I guess we'd better start walking," she said. "It's a long way to Farlow Creek."

The group set off, all of them glancing back from time to time at the growing dome behind them. In the distance, they could see pteranodons flying. It was an alien world in there. But it also contained friends. . . .

Epilogue

LIFE ALWAYS STRIVES to survive. It is one of the traits that is shared by all living creatures. Sometimes the fight ends in failure. Sometimes there is even a second chance. The *dainid* have been given their second chance. But will the human race be able to allow them to live? Or will they want only to kill these survivors of a distant past?

Only time will tell. But then, time always does.

TOR BOOKS

☑ **Check out these titles from**
Award-Winning Young Adult Author
NEAL SHUSTERMAN

Enter a world where reality takes a U-turn...

MindQuakes: Stories to Shatter Your Brain

"A promising kickoff to the series. Shusterman's mastery of suspense and satirical wit make the ludicrous fathomable and entice readers into suspending their disbelief. He repeatedly interjects plausible and even poignant moments into otherwise bizzare scenarios…[T]his all-too-brief anthology will snare even the most reluctant readers."—*Publishers Weekly*

MindStorms: Stories to Blow Your Mind

MindTwisters: Stories that Play with Your Head

And don't miss these exciting stories from Neal Shusterman:

Scorpion Shards

"A spellbinder."—*Publishers Weekly*

"Readers [will] wish for a sequel to tell more about these interesting and unusual characters."—*School Library Journal*

The Eyes of Kid Midas

"Hypnotically readable!"—*School Library Journal*

Dissidents

"An Involving read."—*Booklist*

TOR BOOKS

"A GREAT NEW TALENT. HE BLOWS MY MIND IN A FUN WAY."
—Christopher Pike

Welcome to the PsychoZone.

Where is it? Don't bother looking for it on a map. It's not a place, but a state of mind—a twisted corridor in the brain where reality and imagination collide.

But hold on tight. Once inside the PsychoZone there's no slowing down...and no turning back.

The PsychoZone series by David Lubar

❑ **Kidzilla & Other Tales**
0-812-55880-4 $4.99/$6.50 CAN

❑ **The Witch's Monkey & Other Tales**
0-812-55881-2 $3.99/$4.99 CAN

Call toll-free 1-800-288-2131 to use your major credit card or clip and send this form to order by mail

Send to: Publishers Book and Audio Mailing Service
PO Box 120159, Staten Island, NY 10312-0004

Please send me the books checked above. I am enclosing $_____.
(Please add $1.50 for the first book, and 50¢ for each additional book to cover postage and handling. Send check or money order only—no CODs).

Name _____

Address _____

City _____ State _____ Zip _____